THE

MILLS & BOON®
Centenary Collection

**Celebrating 100 years of romance with
the very best of Mills & Boon**

*First published in Great Britain 2008
by Harlequin Mills & Boon Limited,
Eton House, 18-24 Paradise Road, Richmond, Surrey TW9 1SR*

© Lynne Graham 2001

ISBN: 978 0 263 86648 3

76-0109

*Harlequin Mills & Boon policy is to use papers that are
natural, renewable and recyclable products and made from
wood grown in sustainable forests. The logging and
manufacturing processes conform to the legal environmental
regulations of the country of origin.*

*Printed and bound in Spain
by Litografia Rosés S.A., Barcelona*

The Christmas Eve Bride

by
Lynne Graham

MILLS & BOON
Pure reading pleasure

Lynne Graham was born in Northern Ireland and has been a keen Mills & Boon reader since her teens. She is very happily married with an understanding husband, who has learned to cook since she started to write! Her five children keep her on her toes. She has a very large dog, which knocks everything over, a very small terrier which barks a lot, and two cats. When time allows, Lynne is a keen gardener.

CHAPTER ONE

ROCCO VOLPE was bored and, as it was not a sensation he was accustomed to feeling, he was much inclined to blame his hosts for that reality.

When the banker, Harris Winton, had invited him to his country home for the weekend, Rocco had expected stimulating company. People invariably went to a great deal of trouble to entertain Rocco. But then he could hardly have foreseen that Winton would miss his flight home from Brussels, leaving his unfortunate guests at the mercy of his wife, Kaye.

Kaye, the youthful trophy wife, who looked at Rocco with a hunger she couldn't hide. His startlingly handsome features were expressionless as his hostess irritated him with simpering flattery and far too much attention. He had never liked small women with big eyes, he reflected. Memory stirred, reminding him *why* that was so. Swiftly, he crushed that unwelcome recollection out.

'So tell me…what's it like being one of the most eligible single men in the world?' Kaye asked fatuously.

'Pretty boring.' Watching her redden without remorse, Rocco strolled over to the window like a tiger sheathing his claws with extreme reluctance.

'I suppose it must be,' the beautiful brunette then

agreed in a cloying tone. 'How many men have your power, looks *and* fabulous wealth?'

Striving not to wince while telling himself that if he ever married *his* wife would have a brain, Rocco surveyed the well-kept gardens. Fading winter sunlight gleamed over the downbent head of a gardener raking up leaves on the extensive front lawn. There was something familiar about that unusual honey shade of blonde that was the colour of toffee in certain lights. He stiffened as the figure turned and he realised it was a woman *and*…?

'Your gardener is a woman?' Not a shade of the outraged incredulity and anger consuming Rocco was audible in his deep, dark drawl. But someone ought to warn Winton that he had a potential tabloid spy working for him, he thought grimly. Harris would never recover from the humiliation of the media exposing one of his wife's affairs.

His keen hostess drew level with him and wrinkled her nose. 'We have trouble getting outside staff. Harris says people don't want that kind of work these days.'

'I imagine he's right. Has she been with you long?'

'Only a few weeks.' The brunette studied him with a perplexed frown.

'Will you excuse me? I have an urgent call to make.'

Amber's back was sore.

It was icy cold but the amount of energy she had expended had heated her up to the extent that she was working in a light T-shirt. She could hardly believe that within ten days it would be Christmas. Her honey-blonde hair caught back in a clip from which strands continually drifted loose, she straightened and stretched to ease her complaining spine. About five feet three in height, she was slim, but at breast and hip she was lush and feminine in shape.

It would be another hour before she finished work and she couldn't *wait*. Only a few months back, she would have said she loved the great outdoors, but working for the Wintons had disenchanted her fast. Nothing but endless back-breaking labour and abysmally low pay. Her rich employers did not believe in spending money on labour-saving devices like leaf blowers. On the other hand, Harris Winton was a perfectionist, who demanded the highest standards against impossible odds.

'Brush up the leaves as they fall,' he had told her with a straight face, seeming not to grasp that, with several acres of wooded and lawned grounds, that was like asking her to daily stem an unstoppable tide.

You're turning into a right self-pitying moan, her conscience warned her as she emptied the wheelbarrow. So once she had had nice clothes, pretty, polished fingernails and a career with a future. She might no longer have any of those things but she *did* have Freddy, she reminded herself in consolation.

Freddy, the pure joy in her life, who could squeeze her heart with one smile. Freddy, who had filled her with so much instant love that she could still barely accept the intensity of her own feelings. Freddy, who might not be the best conversationalist yet and who loved to wake her up to play in the middle of the night, but who still made *any* sacrifice worthwhile.

'*Buon giorno*, Amber…what an unexpected pleasure!'

At the sound of that dark, well-modulated voice coming out of nowhere at her, Amber jerked rigid with fright. Blinking rapidly, disbelief engulfing her, she spun round, refusing to accept her instinctive recognition of that rich-accented drawl.

'Strange but somehow extraordinarily *apt* that you should be grubbing round a compost heap,' Rocco remarked with sardonic amusement.

A wave of stark dizziness assailed Amber. As she focused in paralysed incredulity on the formidably tall, well-built male standing beneath the towering beech trees a few yards away, her heart was beating at such an accelerated rate that she could hardly get breath into her lungs. She turned white as milk, every ounce of natural colour evaporating from her fine features, her clear green eyes huge.

Rocco Volpe, the powerful Italian financier, once christened the Silver Wolf by the gossip columns for his breathtaking good looks and fast reputation with her sex. And there was no denying that he *was* spectacular, with his bronzed skin and dark, dark deepset eyes contrasted with hair so naturally, unexpectedly fair it shone like polished silver. Rocco Volpe, the very worst mistake she had made in her twenty-three years of life. Her tummy felt hollow, her every tiny muscle bracing in self-defence. But her brain just refused to snap back into action. She could only wonder in amazement what on earth Rocco Volpe could possibly be doing wandering round the grounds of the Wintons' country house.

'Where did you come from?' she whispered jaggedly.

'The house. I'm staying there this weekend.'

'Oh…' Amber was silenced and appalled by that admission. Yet it was not a remarkable coincidence that Rocco should be acquainted with her employer, for both men wielded power in the same cut-throat world of international finance.

Tilting his arrogant head back, Rocco treated her to a leisurely, all-male appraisal that was as bold as he was. 'Not good news for you, I'm afraid.'

Amber was as stung by that insolent visual assessment as if he had slapped her in the face. *Grubbing round the compost heap?* The instant he bent the full effect of those brilliant dark eyes on her, she recalled that sarcastic comment. But a split second later thought was overpowered by the slowburn effect of Rocco skimming his intense gaze over the swell of her full breasts. Within her bra, the tender peaks of her sensitive flesh pinched tight with stark awareness. As his stirring scrutiny slid lazily down to the all-female curve of her hips, an almost forgotten ache clenched her belly.

'And what's that supposed to mean?' Amber folded her arms with a jerk, holding her treacherous body rigid as if by so doing she might drive out those mortifying responses. Only now she was horribly conscious of her wind-tossed hair, her lack of make-up and her workworn T-shirt and jeans. Once, she recalled, she had taken time to groom herself for Rocco's benefit. Suddenly she wanted to dive into the wretched compost heap and *hide*! Rocco, so smooth, sophisticated and exclusive in his superb charcoal-grey business suit and black cashmere coat. He had to be wondering now what he had *ever* seen in her and her already battered pride writhed under that humiliating suspicion.

'Why are you working for Harris Winton as a gardener?' Rocco asked drily.

'That's none of your business.' Pale and fighting a craven desire to cringe, Amber flung her head high, determined not to be intimidated.

'But I am making it my business,' Rocco countered levelly.

Amber could not credit his nerve. Her temper was rising. 'Being one of the Wintons' guests *doesn't* give you the right to give me the third degree. Now, why don't you go away and leave me alone?'

'You really have changed your tune, *cara*,' Rocco murmured in a tone as smooth as black velvet. 'As I recall, I found persuading *you* to leave *me* alone quite a challenge eighteen months ago.'

That cruel reminder stabbed Amber like a knife in the heart. Indeed, she felt quite sick inside. She had not expected that level of retaliation and dully questioned why. Rocco was a ruthless wheeler-dealer in the money markets and as feared as he was famed for his brilliance. In automatic self-protection from that cutting tongue, she began walking away. Eighteen months ago, Rocco had *dumped* her. Indeed, Rocco had dumped her without hesitation. Rocco had then refused her phone calls and when she had persisted in daring to try and speak to him, he had finally called her back and asked her with icy contempt if she was now 'stalking' him!

'Where are you going?' Rocco demanded.

Amber ignored him. She had been working near the house. Obviously he had seen and recognised her and curiosity had got to him. But it struck her as strange that he should have acted on that curiosity and come outside to speak to her. A guy who had suggested that she might have stalking tendencies ought to have looked the other way. But then that had only been Rocco's brutally effective method of finally shaking her off.

'Amber…'

Bitterness surged up inside her, the destructive bitterness she had believed she had put behind her. But, faced with Rocco again, those feelings erupted back out of her subconscious mind like a volcano. She spun back with knotted fists, her small, shapely figure taut, angry colour warming her complexion. 'I hate you…I can't *bear* to be anywhere near you!'

Rocco elevated a cool, slanting dark brow. He looked hugely unimpressed by that outburst.

'And that is not the reaction of the proverbial woman scorned,' Amber asserted between gritted teeth, determined to disabuse him of any such ego-boosting notion. 'That is the reaction of a woman looking at you now and asking herself how the heck she could ever have been so *stupid* as to get involved with a rat like you!'

Alive with sizzling undertones and tension, the splintering silence almost seemed to shimmer around them. Glittering dark golden eyes flamed into hers in a crash-and-burn collision and she both sensed and saw the fury there that barely showed in that lean, strong face. No, he hadn't liked being called a rat.

'But you'd come back to me like a bullet if I asked you,' Rocco murmured softly.

Amber stared back at him in shock. 'Are you kidding?'

'Only making a statement of fact. But don't get excited,' Rocco advised with silken scorn. 'I'm *not* asking.'

Unfamiliar rage whooshed up inside Amber and she trembled. 'Tell me, are you trying to goad me into physically attacking you?'

'Possibly trying to settle a score or two.' With that unapologetic admission, Rocco studied her with cloaked eyes, his hard bone-structure grim. 'But let's cut to the baseline. You can only be working here to spy on the Wintons for some sleazy tabloid story—'

'I beg…your pardon?' Amber cut in unevenly, her eyes very wide.

Ignoring that interruption, Rocco continued, 'Harris is a friend. I intend to warn him about you—'

'What sleazy tabloid story? Warn him about *me*?' Amber parroted with helpless emphasis. 'Are you out of your mind? I'm not spying on anyone… I'm only the gardener, for goodness' sake!'

'*P-lease,*' Rocco breathed with licking contempt. 'Do I look that stupid?'

Amber was gaping at him while struggling to master her disbelief at his suspicions.

'How much money did you make out of that trashy kiss-and-tell spread on me?' Rocco enquired lazily.

'Nothing…' Amber told him after a sick pause, momentarily drowning in unpleasant recollections of the events which had torn her life apart eighteen months earlier. A couple of hours confiding in an old schoolfriend and the damage had been done. What had seemed like harmless girly gossip had cost her the man she loved, the respect of work colleagues and ultimately her career.

Rocco dealt her a derisive look. 'Do you really think I'm likely to swallow that tale?'

'I don't much care.' And it was true, Amber registered in some surprise. Here she was, finally getting the opportunity to defend herself but no longer that eager to take it. But then the chance had come more than a year too late. A time during which she had been forced to eat more humble pie than was good for her. She had stopped loving him, stopped hoping he would contact her and stopped caring about his opinion of her as well. After he had ditched her, Rocco had delighted the gossip columnists with a series of wild affairs with other women. He had provided her with the most effective cure available for a broken heart. Her pride had kicked in to save her and she had pulled herself together again.

'You already have all the material you need on the Wintons?' Rocco prompted with strong distaste.

The rage sunk beneath the onslaught of sobering memories gripped Amber again. 'Where do you get off, throwing wild accusations like this at me? What gives you the right to ignore what I say and assume that I'm lying? Your *superior* intellect?' Her green eyes flashed bright as emerald jewels in her heart-shaped face, her scorn palpable. 'Well, it's letting you down a bucketful right now, Rocco—'

'My ESP is on overload right now. I don't think so,' Rocco mused, studying her with penetrating cool.

A hollow laugh was wrenched from Amber's dry throat. 'No, you naturally wouldn't think that you could be wrong. After all, you're the guy who's always one hundred per cent right about everything—'

'I wasn't right about you, was I? I got *burned*,' Rocco cut in with harsh clarity, hard facial bones prominent beneath his bronzed skin.

I got burned. Was that how he now viewed their former relationship? Amber was surprised to hear that, but relieved to think that the hurt, the embarrassment and the self-recriminations had not only been hers. But then he was talking about his pride, the no-doubt wounding effect of his conviction that she had somehow contrived to put one over him. He wasn't talking about true emotions, only superficial ones.

'But not enough,' Amber responded tightly, thinking wretchedly of the months of misery she had endured before she'd wised up and got on with her life without looking back to what might have been. 'I don't think you were burned half enough.'

'How the hell could you have expected to hang onto me after what you did?' Rocco demanded with a savage abruptness that disconcerted her. His spectacular eyes rested with keen effect on her surprised face.

'Only two possible explanations, aren't there?' The breeze clawing stray strands of her honey-blonde hair back from her flushed cheekbones, Amber tilted her chin, green eyes sparkling over him where he now stood only feet from her. 'Either I was a dumb little bunny who was indiscreet with an undercover journalist *or*…I was bored out of my tiny mind with you and decided to go out of your life with a big, unforgettable bang!'

'*Dio*…you were *not* bored in my bed,' Rocco growled with raw self-assurance.

Rocco only had to say 'bed' in that dark, accented drawl and heat pulsated through Amber in an alarming wave of reaction and remembrance. Punishing him for her own weakness, she let a stinging smile curve her generous mouth. 'And how would you know, Rocco? Haven't you ever read the statistics on women faking it to keep tender male egos intact?'

The instant those provocative words escaped her, she was shaken by her own unusual venom. But she was even more taken aback by the level to which she had sunk in her instinctive need to deny even the physical hold he had once had on her. Ashamed of herself and furious with him for goading her to that point, she added, 'Look, why don't you just forget you ever saw me out here and we'll call it quits?'

'*Faking* it…' His brilliant dark eyes flared to stormy gold, his Italian accent thick as honey on the vowel sounds of those two words. He had paled noticeably below his bronzed skin and it was that much more noticeable because dark colour now scored his hard masculine cheekbones. 'Were you really?'

Connecting with his glittering look of challenge, Amber felt the primal charge in the atmosphere but she stood her ground, none too proud of her own words but ready to do anything sooner than retract them. He was sexual dynamite and he had to know it. But he need not look to any confirmation of that reality from her. 'All I want to do right now is get on with my work—'

Without the smallest warning, Rocco reached for her arm to prevent her from turning away and flipped her back. 'Was it *work* in my bed too?' he demanded in a savage undertone. 'Did you know right from the start what you were planning to do?'

Backed into the constraining circle of his arms, Amber stared up at him in sensual shock, astonished at the depth of his dark, brooding anger but involuntarily excited by it and by him. Mouth running dry, breath trapped in her throat, she could feel every taut, muscular angle of his big, powerful body against hers. She shivered, conscious of the freezing air on her bare arms but the wanton fire flaming in her pelvis, stroked to the heights by the potent proof of his arousal, recognisable even through the layers of their clothing. The wanting, the helpless, craving hunger that leapt through her in wild response took her by storm.

'I wouldn't touch you again if I was dying...' As swiftly as he had reached for her, Rocco thrust her back from him in contemptuous rejection, strong-boned features hard as iron.

Her fair complexion hotly flushed, Amber turned away in an uncoordinated half-circle, heartbeat racing, legs thoroughly unsteady support. 'Good, so *go*—'

'I'm not finished with you yet.' Leaving those cold words of threat hanging, Rocco strode off.

In a daze, she watched him walk away from her. He had magnificent carriage and extraordinary grace for a male of his size. He soon disappeared from view, screened by the bulky evergreen shrubs flourishing below the winter-bare trees that edged the lawn surrounding the house. Amber only then realised that she was trembling and frozen to the marrow, finally conscious of the chill wind piercing her thin T-shirt. She grabbed her sweater out of the tumbledown greenhouse where she had left it and fumbled into its comforting warmth with hands that were all fingers and thumbs.

What had Rocco meant by saying he wasn't finished

with her yet? She tried to concentrate but it was a challenge because she was so appalled by the way he had made her feel. Suppressing that uneasy awareness, she tensed in even greater dismay. Only minutes ago, he had told her that he intended to warn Harris Winton about the risk that she could be spying on him and his wife in the hope of selling some scandalous story to a newspaper.

Dear heaven, she could not afford to lose her job, for it might not pay well but it *did* include accommodation. Small and basic the cottage might be, but it was the sole reason that Amber had applied to work for the Wintons in the first place. Indeed, the mere thought of being catapulted back into her sister Opal's far more spacious and comfortable home to listen to a chorus of deeply humiliating 'I told you so's' filled Amber with even more horror than the prospect of grovelling to Rocco!

CHAPTER TWO

ROCCO was certain to be lodged in the main suite of the opulent guest wing, Amber reckoned. Just to think that she had probably fixed that huge flower arrangement in there purely for Rocco's benefit made her wince as she headed for the rear entrance to the sprawling country house.

Helping out the Wintons' kindly middle-aged housekeeper, who had been run off her feet preparing for guests the previous month, had resulted in Amber finding herself landed with another duty. The minute that Kaye Winton had realised that their gardener had done the magnificent floral arrangement in the front reception hall, she had demanded that Amber should continue doing creative things with flowers whenever she and her husband entertained.

A time-consuming responsibility that Amber had resented, however, was now welcome as an excuse to enter the house. How on earth could she have let Rocco take off on that chilling threat? His suspicions about her were ridiculous, but she knew *why* he believed the Wintons might be the target for media interest of the most unpleasant kind. Harris Winton was an influential man, who was often in the news. But, for goodness' sake, the whole neighbourhood, never mind the staff, knew about Kaye Winton's extra-marital forays!

Sometimes, men were so naïve, Amber reflected ruefully. A newspaper reporter would only need to stop off in the village post office to hear chapter and verse on the voracious brunette's far-from-discreet affairs!

Catering staff were bustling about the big kitchen. Leaving her muddy work boots in the passage and removing the clip from her hair to finger-comb it into a hopeful state of greater tidiness, Amber hurried up the stone service staircase in her sock soles. With a bit of luck, Rocco would be in his suite. If he was downstairs, what was she going to do? Leave him some stupid note begging him to be reasonable? Grimacing at that idea, Amber wondered angrily why Rocco was allowing his usual cool common sense and intelligence to be over-powered by melodramatic assumptions.

I got burned. Well, if Rocco imagined the slight mortification of that newspaper spread on their affair eighteen months back had been the equivalent of getting burned, she would have liked him to have had a taste of what she had suffered in comparison. Her life, her self-respect and her dreams had gone down the drain faster than floodwater.

In the guest wing, she knocked quietly on the door of the main suite. There was no answer but, as she was aware that several rooms lay beyond and Rocco might be in any one of them, she went in and eased the door closed behind her again. She heard his voice then. It sounded as if he was on the phone and she approached the threshold of the bedroom with hesitant steps.

Rocco's brilliant dark eyes struck her anxious gaze and she froze. Clearly, he had heard both her initial knock and her subsequent entrance uninvited. Her skin heated with discomfiture when, with a fluid gesture of mocking invitation, he indicated the sofa several feet from him. He continued with his call, his rich dark drawl wrapping round mellow Italian syllables with a sexy musicality that sent tiny little shivers of recall down her taut spinal cord. She recognised a couple of words, recalled how she had once planned to learn his language. With a covert rub of her damp palms on her worn jeans, she sat down, stiff with strain. He lounged by the window, talking into his mobile phone, bold, bronzed features in profile, his attention removed from her.

He stood about six feet four and he had the lean muscular build of an athlete. Broad shoulders, narrow hips, long, long powerful legs. His clothes were always beautifully tailored and cut to fit him like a glove. Yet he could look elegant clad only in a towel, she recalled uneasily from the past. Her colour rising afresh at the tone of her thoughts, she looked away, conscious of the tremor in her hands, the tension licking through her smaller, slighter frame.

They had been together for three months when Rocco had ditched her. For her, anyway, it had been love at first sight. He had called her 'tabbycat' because of the way she had used to curl up on the sofa beside him. When he had been out of the country over weekends and holidays, he had flown her out to join him in a variety of exotic places. Her feet hadn't touched the ground once during their magical affair. All her innate caution and sense had fallen by the wayside. Finding herself on a roller coaster of excitement and passion, she had become enslaved. When the roller coaster had come to a sudden halt and thrown her off, she had not been able to credit that he'd been able to just abandon what *she* had believed they had shared.

That was why she had kept on phoning him at first, accepting that he was furious with her about that ghastly newspaper story, accepting that that story had been entirely her fault and that *she* had had to be the one to make amends. Loving Rocco had taught her how to be humble and face her mistakes.

And how had he rewarded her humility? He had kicked her in the teeth! Her delicate bone-structure tightened. She pushed her honey-blonde hair off her brow, raking it back, so that it tumbled in glossy disarray round her slim shoulders. Her hair needed cutting: she was letting it grow because it was cheaper. At the rate that her finances were improving, she thought ruefully, she would have hair down to her feet by the time she could afford a salon appointment again. Loving Rocco had also taught her what it was like to be poor…or, at least, how utterly humiliating it was, after a long period of independence, to be forced to rely once more on family generosity to survive.

Her tummy churning with nerves, she focused on Rocco again, noting the outline of his long, luxuriant black lashes, comparing them to Freddy's… Freddy's hair was as dark as Rocco's was fair, black as a raven's wing. She squeezed her eyes tight shut and prayed for concentration and courage.

'To what do I owe the honour of this second meeting?' Rocco enquired drily. 'I thought we were just about talked out.'

Worrying at her lower lip, Amber tilted her head back. But she could still only see as high as his gold silk tie because he had moved closer. In a harried movement, she stood up again. 'If you tell Harris Winton that there is the slightest possibility that I might be spying on him for some newspaper, I'll get the sack!'

Rocco studied her with inscrutable dark eyes. In the charged silence that he allowed to linger, his lean, powerful face remained impassive.

'I can't understand why you should even *think* such a thing of me…it's nonsensical!'

'Is it? I remember you telling me that you once very much wanted to *be* a journalist...'

Amber stilled in consternation and surprise. *Had* she told Rocco that? During one of those trusting chats when he had seemed to want to know every tiny thing about her? Evidently, she had told him but she hadn't given him the whole picture. During her teens, Amber's parents had put her under constant pressure to produce better exam results and, when they'd finally realised that she was not going to become a doctor, a lawyer or a teacher, she had been instructed to focus on journalism instead. They had signed her up for an extra-curricular media studies course on which she had got very poor grades.

'*And* how desperately disappointed you were when you couldn't get a job on a newspaper,' Rocco finished smoothly.

For the first time it occurred to Amber that, eighteen months back, Rocco had had more reason than she had appreciated to believe that the prospect of media limelight might have tempted her into talking about their relationship. She was furious that one insignificant little piece of information casually given out of context could have helped to support his belief that she was guilty as charged.

'Do you know the only reason I went for that job? My parents had just died... It was *their* idea that I should try for a career in journalism, not my own. And what I might or might not have wanted at the age of sixteen has very little bearing on the person I am now,' Amber declared in driven dismissal.

Rocco continued to regard her in level challenge. 'I can concede that. But when we met, you were employed in a merchant bank and studying for accountancy exams. Give me one good reason why you should now be pretending to be a gardener?'

'Because, obviously, it's *not* a pretence! It's the only job I could get…at least the only work that it's convenient for me to take right now.' In a nervous gesture as she tacked on that qualification, Amber half opened her hands and then closed them tight again, her green eyes veiling, for the last thing she wanted to touch on was the difficulties of being a single parent on a low wage.

'Convenient?' Rocco queried.

'I live in a cottage in the coachyard here. Accommodation goes with the job. My sister lives nearby and I like being close to her—'

'You never mentioned that you *had* a sister while I was with you.'

Amber flushed a dull guilty red for she had allowed him to assume that she was as alone in the world as he was. Rocco was an only child, born to older parents, who had both passed away by the time he'd emerged from his teens.

'So explain why you kept quiet about having a sister,' Rocco continued levelly.

But there was no way Amber felt she could tell him the honest truth on that score. She had been terrified that Rocco would meet her gorgeous, intellectual big sister and start thinking of Amber herself as very much a poor second best. It had happened before, after all. It didn't matter that Opal was twelve years older and happily married. People were always amazed when they learnt that the highly successful barrister, Opal Carlton, was Amber's sibling. From an early age, Amber had been aware that she was a sad disappointment to her parents, who, being so clever themselves, had expected equally great things from their younger daughter as well. Her best had never, ever been good enough.

'Well, I have a sister and I'm very fond of her,' she mumbled, not meeting his eyes because she was ashamed that she had kept Opal hidden like a nasty secret when indeed she could not have got through the past year without her sister's support.

'Why are you feeding me this bull?' Rocco demanded with sardonic bite. 'Nothing you've said so far comes anywhere near explaining why you should suddenly be clutching a wheelbarrow instead of fingering a keyboard!'

Amber swallowed hard. 'Within a month of that kiss-and-tell story appearing in print, I was at the top of the hit list at Woodlawn Wyatt. They said they were over-staffed and, along with some others, I lost my job.'

'That doesn't surprise me,' Rocco conceded without sympathy. 'Merchant banks are conservative institutions—'

'And the regular banks are still shedding staff practically by the day so I couldn't find another opening,' Amber admitted, tight-mouthed, hating the necessity of letting him know that she had struggled but failed to find similar employment. 'I also suspect that, whenever a reference *was* taken up with my former employers, the knives came out—'

'Possibly,' Rocco mused in the same noncommittal tone. 'But had you stayed in London—'

'Being out of work in a big city is expensive. I hadn't been with Woodlawn Wyatt long enough to qualify for a redundancy payment. I moved in with my sister for a while—'

'This is a rural area but it's also part of the commuter belt. Surely you could have found employment *more*—'

Her patience gave out. 'Look, I'm happy as I am and I only came up here in the first place to ask you to back off and just forget you ever saw me!'

Rocco lounged back against the polished footboard on the elegant sleigh bed, bringing their eyes into

sudden direct contact and somehow making her awe-
somely aware that they were in a bedroom together. 'Do
you really mean that?'

Amber blinked but it didn't break the mesmerising
hold of his arresting dark golden eyes for long enough
to stifle the terrifying tide of sheer physical longing
that washed over her. Memory was like a cruel hook
dragging her down into a dangerous undertow of
intimate images she was already fighting not to recall.
Rocco tumbling her down on his bed and kissing her
with the explosive force that charged her up with the
passion she had never been able to resist; Rocco's expert
hands roving over her to waken her in the morning; the
sheer joy of being wanted more than she had ever been
wanted by anyone in her entire life.

'What are you t-talking about?' Amber stammered,
dredging herself out of those destabilising and enervating memories.

'Do you really want me to forget I ever saw you?'
Rocco viewed her steadily from beneath inky black
lashes longer than her own.

'What else?' Already conscious of her heightened
colour and quickened breathing, Amber was very still for
every fibre of her being was awake to the smouldering
atmosphere that had come up out of nowhere to entrap her.

'Liar…' The effect of the husky reproof Rocco delivered was infinitely less than the sudden sensual smile
of amusement that curled his wide, eloquent mouth.

Images from a distant, happier past assailed Amber:
the sound of a smile in his deep voice on the phone, the
feeling of euphoria, of being appreciated when he looked
at her in just that way. What way? As if there were only
the two of them in the whole wide world, as if she was
someone *special*. Before Rocco came along, nobody had
ever made Amber feel special or important or needed.

Her breath catching in her throat, she stared back at him, wholly enchanted by the charisma of that breathtaking smile. 'I'm not lying…' she muttered without even being aware of what she was saying.

Rocco reached out and closed his hands over hers. At first contact, a helpless shiver ran through her. Slowly, he smoothed out her tightly clenched fingers, one by one. Like a rabbit caught in car headlights, she gazed up at him, heart banging against her ribcage, aware only of him and the seductive weakness induced by the heat blossoming inside her. He eased her inches closer. His warmth, the feel of his skin on hers again, the powerful intoxicant of his familiar scent overpowered her senses.

'I said I wouldn't touch you again if I was dying *but*…' The rasp of his voice travelled down her responsive spine like hot, delicious honey.

'But?'

'*Dio*…' Rocco husked, drawing her the last couple of inches. 'I believe I could be persuaded otherwise, tabbycat…'

The sound of that endearment made her melt.

'However, you would have to promise to keep it quiet—'

'Quiet?' All concentration shot, she didn't grasp what he was talking about.

'I don't want to open a newspaper on Monday morning to find out how I scored between the sheets again—'

'Sorry…?'

Without warning, Rocco released her hands and, since he was just about all that was holding her upright on her wobbling lower limbs, she almost fell on top of him. He righted her again with deft cool. 'Think about it,' he advised, stepping away from her.

For an instant, Amber hovered, breathing in deep,

striving to get her brain into gear again. She did not have to think very hard. 'Apart from the obvious, what are you trying to imply?'

'I'm bored this weekend and you challenged me.'

In considerable emotional disarray as she appreciated that she had been standing there transfixed and hypnotised, entirely entrapped by the sexual power he had exercised over her, Amber spun round. 'I beg your pardon?'

Rocco sent her a sizzling glance of mockery. 'Maybe I want to see you *faking* it for my benefit.'

Amber reddened to the roots of her hair. 'No chance,' she said curtly and stepped past him to hurry back out to the sitting room.

Without the slightest warning whatsoever, the door she was heading for opened and Kaye Winton walked in. At the sight of Amber, she frowned in astonishment, pale blue eyes rounding. 'What are you doing up here?'

Mind a complete blank, Amber found herself glancing in desperation at Rocco.

Brilliant dark eyes gleaming, Rocco said, 'I asked for someone to remove the flowers.'

'The flowers?' the beautiful brunette questioned.

'I'm allergic to them.' Rocco told the lie with a straight face.

'Oh, no!' Kaye surged over to the centre table as if jet-propelled. Gathering up the giant glass vase, she planted it bodily into Amber's hastily extended arms. 'Take them away immediately. I'm so sorry, Rocco!'

Her sweater soaked by the water that had slopped out of the vase with the other woman's careless handling, Amber headed for the corridor at speed, her shaken expression hidden by the mass of trendy corkscrew twigs and lilies she had arranged earlier that day. It was ironic that she should be grateful for Rocco's quick thinking, even more relieved that her employer's wife had not come in a minute sooner and found her in his bedroom. How on earth would she ever have explained that?

Indeed, how could she even explain to *herself* why she had allowed Rocco to behave as he had? She had acted like a doll without mind or voice and offered no objection to his touching her. Sick with shame at her own weakness, Amber disposed of the floral arrangement and pulled on her work boots again with unsteady hands. Rocco was bored. Rocco was playing manipulative games with her to amuse himself. Dear heaven, that *hurt* her so much. And she knew it shouldn't hurt, knew she should have been fully on her guard and capable of resisting Rocco's smouldering sexuality.

Wasn't she supposed to hate him? Well, hatred had kept her far from cool when he'd turned up the heat. And there she was blaming him when she ought to be blaming herself! Rocco had made her want him again…instantly, easily, reawakening the hunger she had truly believed she had buried for ever. But with every skin-cell alight with anticipation, she had just been desperate for him to kiss her. And he hadn't kissed her either, which told her just how complete his own control had been in comparison to her own.

Well, she was going to spend the rest of the weekend at her sister's house and stay well out of Rocco's way, she told herself impulsively. Then she recalled that she *couldn't* do that. True, she was babysitting at her sister's that evening, but she had to work Saturdays and would have to turn in as usual. Harris Winton was usually home only at weekends and the reason Amber got a day off mid-week instead was that her employer insisted that she be available for his weekly inspection tour of the grounds.

She trudged round to the old coachyard and climbed into the ten-year-old hatchback her brother-in-law,

Neville, had given her on loan, saying it had been a trade-in for one of the luxury cars he imported, but not really convincing her with that less-than-likely story. Furthermore, the car was on permanent loan, Amber reflected heavily, once again reminded of just how dependent she *was* on Neville and Opal's generosity.

The independence she had sought was as far out of her reach as it had ever been, she conceded heavily. Her sole source of pride was that she was no longer living under her sister's roof. But she was only able to work because she shared the services of the expensive but very well-trained nanny her sister employed to look after her own child. Amber's low salary would not stretch to full-time childcare or indeed towards much of a contribution towards the nanny's salary. So she kept on saying thank you to her family and accepting for Freddy's sake, striving to repay their generosity by making herself useful in other ways. It occurred to her then that she could have wiped the sardonic smile from Rocco's darkly handsome features with just a few words.

As she drove over to the exclusive housing development where her sister lived, she asked herself why she hadn't spoken those words to Rocco when she had finally got the opportunity.

'Rocco Volpe is pond scum,' her sister, Opal, had pronounced on the day of Freddy's birth. 'But I'd sooner cut my throat than watch you humiliate yourself trailing him through the courts to establish paternity and win a financial settlement. Rich men fight paternity suits every step of the way. The whole process can drag on for years, particularly when the father is not a British citizen. He could leave the country and stonewall you at every turn. Keep your pride…that's my advice.'

Her pride? The very thought of telling Rocco that she

had given birth to his child flicked Amber's pride on the raw. Rocco had pulled no punches when he'd ended their relationship. Amber's troubled thoughts took her back in time an entire eighteen months. Had she had proper pride and sense, she would never have got as far as a first date with Rocco Volpe…

CHAPTER THREE

WHEN she was seventeen, Amber had started work as clerk in an accountant's office. She had gratefully accepted the offer of day release and evening classes to study for accounting qualifications; it had been four years before she'd moved on. At twenty-one she had applied for and got a job at the merchant bank, Woodlawn Wyatt, where she had become second in command in the accounts department; her salary had doubled overnight.

'You're the token woman,' her section senior had told her patronisingly.

But Amber hadn't cared that she'd had to work with a male dinosaur, angry that his own choice of candidate had been passed over. Finally having got her foot onto a promising career ladder with that timely move and promotion, she had been happy to work long hours. Busy, busy, busy, that was what she had been, little time for friends or a man in her life, falling into bed exhausted night after night, driven by a desperate need to prove herself and terrified of failing.

She had met Rocco when Woodlawn Wyatt had thrown a big party for the outgoing managing director. Sitting with a fixed smile during the speeches, she had surreptitiously been drawing up a study schedule on a napkin in preparation for her next exam. She had not even noticed Rocco at the top table and when the lights had lowered and the dancing had begun, she had been on the brink of going home, having made her duty appearance.

'Would you like to dance?'

Rocco came out of nowhere at her. She looked up with a frown, only to be stunned by the effect of those spectacular tawny eyes of his. 'Sorry…who are you speaking to?' she mumbled, not crediting for one moment that it might be her.

'You…' Rocco told her gently.

'I don't dance…I was about to leave, actually—'

'Just one dance—'

'I've got two left feet,' she muttered, getting all flustered. 'Did one of my colleagues put you up to this for a joke?'

'Why would anyone do that?'

As it was her responsibility to keep a choke hold on business expense claims, Amber knew herself to be disliked by executive personnel, who loathed the way she pursued them for receipts and explanations of extraordinary bills. It was an unpopular job but she told herself that she wouldn't be doing it for ever.

Embarrassed then by the low self-esteem she had betrayed with her foolish question, she found herself grasping Rocco's extended hand and rising. And from that moment, her safe world started tilting and shifting and becoming an unrecognisable place of sudden colour and emotion. Nothing that followed was within her conscious control. After midnight, she left the party with him, aware of the shaken eyes following in their wake, but it had truly been as if Rocco had cast a spell over her. She had *still* been with Rocco at lunchtime the following day.

'What attracted you to me?' she had asked him once, still mystified.

'My ego couldn't take not being noticed by the one woman in the room worth looking at?'

'Seriously…'

'You had your shoes off under the table and you have these dinky little feet and I went weak with lust—'

'Rocco'

'I took one look and I wanted you chained to my bed, day and night.'

Had she initially been a refreshing novelty to a so-phisticated male accustomed to much more experienced women? Sinking back to the present, Amber parked at the rear of her sister's big detached house and went inside. As they often did, her sister and brother-in-law were staying on in London to go out for the evening with friends before returning home. Amber was booked to babysit as it was their nanny Gemma's night off.

The red-headed nanny was sitting in the airy conservatory with the children. Amber's two-year-old niece, Chloe, was bashing the life out of an electronic teaching toy while Freddy sat entranced by both the racket and the flashing lights.

Freddy…with the single exception of hair colour, Freddy was Rocco in miniature, Amber conceded. He had black hair, big dark golden brown eyes and olive skin. She studied her smiling baby son with eyes that were suddenly stinging. She loved Freddy so much and already he was holding his arms up for her to lift him. As Gemma greeted her while attempting to distract Chloe from the ear-splitting noise she was creating, Amber crouched down and scooped Freddy up. In just over a week, when Christmas arrived, Freddy would be a year old. She drank in the warm, familiar scent of his hair, holding his solid little body close to her own, grateful that she didn't need to worry about taking him back to her cottage at the Wintons' for at least another twenty-four hours.

'You're very quiet. Don't tell me you're still worrying about your car not starting,' her brother-in-law, Neville, scolded as he dropped her off in the cobbled coachyard at the Wintons' early the following morning. 'Look, I'll have that old banger of yours back on the road by this lunchtime. One of my delivery drivers will run it over here for you.'

Sheathed in the fancy black designer dress that she had borrowed from her sister's dry-cleaning bag because she had forgotten to pack for her overnight stay the evening before, Amber climbed out of Neville's Mercedes sports car, and gave him a pained smile. 'Yes, as if it's not bad enough that I have to drag you out of bed on a Saturday morning to take me to work, I now wreck the *rest* of your day by sentencing you to play car mechanic—'

The older man gave her a wry grin. 'Give over, Amber. I'm never happier than when I'm under the bonnet of a car!'

Yeah, sure, Amber thought, guiltily unconvinced as he drove off again. Maybe that was true if the car was a luxury model, but she could not credit that a male who owned as successful a business as Neville did could possibly enjoy working on an old banger. Barefoot and bare-legged because she hadn't wanted to risk waking her sleeping sister by going in search of shoes and underwear to borrow, a bulk, heavy carrier bag containing the previous day's clothes weighing down her arm, Amber rummaged for her keys for the cottage.

She got the fright of her life when a slight sound alerted her to the fact that she had company. Head flying up, she focused in astonishment on Rocco as he stepped into view out of the shadowy recesses behind one of the open archways fronting the coachyard. Casually, if exclusively clad in a husky brown cashmere jacket and tailored beige chinos, luxuriant silver fair hair tousled in the breeze above his devastingly attractive dark features, Rocco literally sent her composure into a downward tailspin.

'So it's *true*,' Rocco pronounced with grim emphasis. 'You've got a middle-aged man in a Merc in tow.'

The hand Amber had extended towards the keyhole on the cottage door fell back limp to her side. 'What are you d-doing out here at this hour?' she stammered, wide-eyed, still to come to grips with his first staggering statement.

Rocco vented a humourless laugh. 'You should know I never lie in bed unless I've got company—'

'But it's barely eight in the morning.' Amber didn't really know why she was going on about the actual time. She only knew that she was so taken aback by Rocco's sudden appearance and her own inability to drag her eyes from that lean, darkly handsome face that she couldn't think straight.

'I've been waiting for you. I want to know if what Kaye Winton said about you after dinner last night was a windup,' Rocco bit out flatly, raking brooding dark eyes over the short fitted dress she wore, lingering in visible disbelief on her incongruously bare legs and feet. '*Dio mio*…he chucks you out of the car half naked in the middle of winter. Where have you been? In a layby somewhere?'

Shivering now in the brisk breeze, Amber was nonetheless welded to the spot, frowning at him in complete incredulity. 'What Kaye Winton *said* about me? What did *she* say about me?'

'She warned me to watch out for you coming onto me as you were the local sex goddess…only she got rather carried away and didn't manage to put it quite that politely.'

Amber's generous lips parted and stayed parted. 'Say that again…' she finally whispered shakily when she was capable of emerging from the severe shock he had dealt her with that bombshell.

'I believe you enjoy a constant procession of different men in flashy expensive cars and regular overnight absences…' Rocco grated in seething disgust, striding forward to snatch her keys from her loosened grasp and open the door. 'Go inside…you're blue with cold!'

'That's an absolute lie!' Amber exclaimed.

Rocco planted a hand to her rigid shoulder and thrust her indoors, following her in to slam the door closed again in his wake. 'I think it's past time you told me what's going *on* with you—'

Amber flung down her carrier bag and rounded on him. 'Now, let me get this straight…Kaye Winton *told* you—'

'After what I've seen with my own eyes I wouldn't swallow a denial,' Rocco cut in angrily. 'So don't waste your breath. Are you hooking to support some kind of life-threatening habit?'

Amber closed her eyes, outraged and appalled that he should even suggest such a thing. 'Are you insane that you can ask me that?'

Rocco closed his hands over hers and pulled her closer. 'Amber, I want the truth. I was tempted to close my hands round that vicious shrew's throat last night and squeeze hard to silence her! I honestly thought it was sheer bitching I was listening to—'

'I want to hear this again. In front of witnesses, that woman—'

'*No* witnesses…the other guests were at the far end of the room when she chose to get confidential—'

Only a little of Amber's growing rage ebbed at that clarification. 'Right, I'll have it out with her face to face—'

'It would be wiser to keep quiet than encourage her to spread such tales further afield—'

Amber lifted angry hands and tried to break his hold. 'Let me go, Rocco. I'm going to tip that dirty-minded besom out of her bed *and*—'

Rocco held fast to her. 'Looking like you're just home from a rough night at a truck stop, that will be *so* impressive!'

'How dare you talk to me like that? How dare you suggest that I might be…that I might be a whore?' Tears that were as much the result of distress as fury lashing her eyes, Amber slung those words back at him with the outrage of raw sincerity.

'I'm sorry if I've offended and hurt you, but I need to know.' Releasing her with relief unconcealed in his brilliant dark incisive eyes, Rocco expelled his breath in a stark hiss. 'So when *did* you get into men in the plural just for fun?'

Amber swept up the jampot of dying wild flowers on the small pine table and flung it at him. The glass jar hit the stainless steel sink several feet behind him and smashed, spattering shards all over the work surface.

'That was buck stupid when you have no shoes on,' Rocco pointed out with immense and galling cool.

'I wish it had hit you!' Amber launched wildly, but the truth was that she was already calming down out of shock at what she had done. She breathed in slow and deep. 'I don't have any life-threatening habits to support either…have you got that straight?'

'I'm very pleased to hear it. But I do wish you had retained the same exclusive attitude to sex.'

Ignoring that acid response, Amber fought to get a

grip on her floundering emotions and understand why Kaye Winton, who had never demonstrated the slightest interest in her private life but whose husband bought their cars through Neville's business, should have muddied her reputation in such an inexcusable way. Had the other woman somehow sensed in Rocco's suite the day before that more was going on between Amber and Rocco than she had seen? Amber had never subscribed to the general local belief that Kaye Winton was an air-head. That might well be the impression the brunette preferred to give around men, but Amber was unconvinced and, recalling the manner in which she herself had automatically looked at Rocco for an inspiring excuse or being found upstairs with him, she suppressed a groan.

'I bet Kaye Winton noticed the way I glanced at you for support yesterday. Strangers don't do that.' Amber sighed. 'But as for the rest of her nonsense…'

It only then occurred to Amber that it was true that she spent regular nights away from the cottage and that it was equally true that she might often have been seen climbing in and out of different cars. Between them, Neville and Opal owned five luxury vehicles. Neville often picked her up on his way home if she was coming over to stay and just as often dropped her back in the morning. Someone watching from an upstairs window would not be able to tell that the driver was always the same man. Even so, she was shattered by the apparent interpretation the brunette had put on what she had seen, yet surprised that the other woman did *not* appear to have mentioned that Amber was also an unmarried mother.

Amber breathed in so deep, her full breasts strained against the fabric of her sister's dress which was too snug a fit under that pressure. She glanced across the room. Rocco had his attention riveted to her chest. She reddened, feeling the sudden heaviness of her own swelling flesh, the tautening of her sensitive nipples. 'Stop it…' she muttered fiercely before she could think better of it.

'Tell me *how*…' Rocco invited in a raw undertone, fabulous cheekbones taut and scoured with colour, eyes like burning golden arrows of challenge on her lovely face.

'I need to get dressed for work—'

'Or you could get *undressed* for me. In fact, you don't need to move a muscle,' Rocco murmured roughly as he closed the distance between them. 'I'll do it for you—'

'But—'

He caught her into the circle of his strong arms and she gazed up at him, heart beating fast and furious in the slight hiatus that followed. She told herself to break away but somehow she did precisely nothing. He lifted her up against him with easy strength. She wrapped her arms round him. He meshed one fierce, controlling hand into the fall of her honey-blonde hair and brought their mouths into hungry devouring collision.

It was like being shot to sudden vibrant life after a long time in suspended animation. With a strangled gasp of shock at the intensity of sensation surging through her quivering frame, she kissed him back with a kind of wild, clumsy, hanging-on-tight desperation. If she stopped to breathe, she might die of deprivation, she might stop *feeling* everything she had thought she would never feel again. A soaring excitement thrummed low in her pelvis, awakening the dulled ache of a physical craving way beyond anything she could control.

But, breathing raggedly, Rocco dragged his expert

sensual mouth from hers and stared down into her shaken green eyes with febrile force. 'You're wearing next to *nothing* under that dress—'

Aghast that he had realised that reality, for she had scarcely clothed herself for entertaining, Amber mumbled in severe discomfiture, 'Well…er—'

Rocco dumped her down on a hard chair by the table. 'How many ways did he have you in the Merc? And when the hell did you turn into such a tramp?' he ground out wrathfully.

'For your information, that was my brother-in-law driving that car!' Amber shot at him furiously.

'Tips you out barefoot at dawn on a regular basis, does he?'

'When my car breaks down and I've spent the night at my sister's home…*yes!*' Amber hissed back. 'And I wasn't going to put a pair of dirty workman's boots on with this dress *and* without clean socks, was I?'

'I suppose all these guys in the expensive cars you've been seen in are married to *sisters* of yours?' Shooting her a look of splintering derision, pallor spread round his ferociously compressed mouth, Rocco strode to the door.

'Two minutes ago, you didn't much care!' Amber heard herself throw at his powerful back in retaliation.

Rocco swung back and surveyed her with shimmering golden eyes. '*Per meraviglia*…who was it who called a halt? I didn't come here to get laid—'

Enraged by that assurance, Amber threw herself upright again. 'I'm still waiting to hear why you did come here because I sure as heck didn't want you anywhere near me!'

'Then isn't it strange that you should find it so difficult to say that one little word, "no"?'

Amber paled and turned away, biting her lip to prevent

herself from making some empty response which would only prolong her own agony of mortification.

'After what I heard last night, I was concerned about you—'

Amber whirled back. '*You* concerned about *me*? Give me a break!'

Rocco stared at her with cold, dark eyes of censure. 'I would do as much for any ex if I thought they needed a helping hand. And don't curl your lip like that. I'm serious,' he spelt out with chilling cool. 'If you need financial help to get yourself out of what appears to be a crisis period in your life, I'll give it to you…no questions asked and *nothing* expected in return.'

The silence hung there like a giant sheet of glass waiting to crash and smash when the seething tension broke. She stared back fixedly at him. A shaken and hollow laugh was wrenched from her convulsed throat. 'So where were you, Rocco…when I *really* needed you?'

A tiny muscle pulled tight at the corner of his expressive mouth and he did not pretend not to follow her meaning. 'I was very angry with you eighteen months ago—'

'*So* angry you couldn't even take a phone call?' Amber squeezed out the reminder with burning bitterness.

His lean, powerful face clenched. 'You knew how much I valued my privacy. I won't apologise for that. You destroyed us when you decided to share salacious details of our relationship with a muck-raking journalist. I could never have trusted you again after that.'

'I gave no salacious details whatsoever, but those sort of details are fairly easily guessed when it comes to a guy with your reputation…and I did not *know* I was talking to a journalist—'

'Amber,' Rocco incised flatly, 'I don't know what you're trying to prove but it's way too late to make the attempt.'

But whose fault was it that it was now too late for her to speak in her own defence? Hatred as savage as the hunger he had roused only minutes earlier flamed into being inside her. 'I'll never forget what you did to me back then,' she said without any expression at all, her heart-shaped face pale but composed. 'You're right. It's way too late to discuss any of that now. Go on…take your precious charity and your nauseatingly pious offer of help out of here and don't you dare come back!'

Stubborn as a rock and contrary in the face of an invitation he should have been all too keen to take in the circumstances, Rocco stood his ground. 'I wasn't being pious and I wasn't offering you charity.'

'You're talking down to me, though, and I won't stand anyone doing that to me.'

'Better that than dragging you back into bed,' Rocco murmured in a savage undertone that shook her as he yanked open the door again.

'I wouldn't *go* to bed with you again!'

His arrogant silvery fair head turned back to her, a searing sexual hunger blatant in the all-encompassing appraisal he gave her. 'If it's any consolation, no woman ever gave me as much pleasure as you—'

'Consolation?' Amber almost choked on that mortifying word and what followed very nearly sent her into orbit with frustrated rage.

'But I need a woman to be exclusively mine—'

'Only you're not so scrupulous yourself,' Amber heard herself remark. 'After you dumped me, according to the gossip columns you were like a sex addict on the loose!'

Taken aback, Rocco froze, and then he sent her a

smouldering look of what could only be described as sheer loathing.

Reeling in shock from that revealing appraisal, Amber went white and she could not drag her stricken gaze from his lean, strong face. 'Rocco…?' she whispered unsteadily.

'*You* did that to me,' he imparted with savage condemnation.

The door thudded shut on his departure, leaving her trembling and in more confusion and turmoil than she had ever thought to experience again.

CHAPTER FOUR

AN HOUR later, just as Amber was ready to go outside and start work, a brisk knock sounded on the cottage door.

She was stunned to find Kaye Winton waiting outside. The brunette, clad in a skin-tight green leather skirt suit, her beautiful face stiff, took advantage of Amber's surprise and strolled in uninvited.

'I'm going to lay this on the line,' Kaye told her curtly. 'If I catch you coming on to one of our guests again, I'll inform my husband.'

Amber gave her an incredulous look. 'Coming *on* to one—?'

'Rocco Volpe. Oh, I don't blame you. In your position I might have done the same. Rocco's a real babe and some catch,' Kaye cut in with a tight little smile, green as grass with envy and resentment. 'But you needn't think I didn't work out that when I interrupted you both yesterday, you were walking out of his bedroom—'

Amber found herself in the very awkward position of being guilty as charged on that count of inappropriate behaviour. And while she had initially intended to confront the other woman about the hatchet job done on her own reputation, nothing was quite that simple.

Admitting that Rocco had repeated the brunette's allegations to her would reveal that Amber was much more intimate with Rocco Volpe than she was prepared to admit. Indeed, so fraught was the entire situation with the risk that she could end up losing her job or, at the very least, be forced into making personal confidences in her own defence, Amber had not yet decided what to do for best.

'Mrs Winton, I—'

'I did my best to limit the damage last night and turn his attention away from you,' Kaye revealed, surprising Amber with that blunt admission. 'When all's said and done, Rocco's just another testosterone-charged bloke on the lookout for sexual variety, but he's *not* going to find it with our gardener. Is that quite clear?'

'I believe you've made yourself very clear,' Amber said grittily, fingernails biting into her palms to restrain her from saying anything she might later come to regret.

The other woman nudged the tiny toy train lying on the tiled floor by the table with the toe of her stiletto-heeled shoe. 'I forgot about your kid…where do you keep him, anyway? Does he only visit you? Now that I think about it, I've never laid eyes on him.'

'I'm sure you're not interested.' Having wondered why Kaye had neglected to inform Rocco that Amber had a baby, Amber concealed her relief at the casual admission that the other woman had simply forgotten Freddy's existence. It was hardly surprising, though, when at the outset of her employment Harris Winton had warned her that he didn't expect to see her using the grounds of the house outside working hours.

Kaye shrugged her agreement. 'You're taking this well—'

'Maybe…maybe not.'

Opening the door again, the brunette dealt her a wry

glance. 'I've done you a favour. My husband would have sacked you yesterday. Harris has Victorian values on staff behaviour.'

Since it was a well-known fact that Kaye Winton had once been a lowly groom working at the riding stables owned by her husband's first wife, Amber could barely swallow that closing comment.

'Men...' Kaye laughed in frank acknowledgement of that hypocrisy. 'Can't live *with* them, can't live without them!'

It was noon when Kaye's husband, Harris, finally came in search of Amber. A small, spare man with a very precise manner, he was much quieter than usual and he cut short his usual lengthy inspection tour by pointing out that he had guests staying. As the rain was coming on heavily by then, Amber was unsurprised at his eagerness to head back indoors again. Resigning herself to a day spent skidding on muddy lawns and getting soaked to the skin, for the rain always found its way through her jacket eventually, Amber got on with her work. Around lunchtime she went back to the cottage and made herself a sandwich before returning outside.

Never had she been more conscious of the vast gulf that had opened up between herself and Rocco. There he was snug indoors on his fancy country-house weekend, being waited on hand and foot, entertained, fed like a king by special caterers and lusted over by his shapely hostess. And here *she* was, in the most subservient of positions with a list of instructions from her employer that she would be lucky to complete in the space of a month, never mind over the next week!

In addition, Rocco *hated* her. So why was that making her feel as if the roof of the world had fallen in around her? She relived that look of his at the outset of the day…violent loathing. She shivered. He went out pulling women as if he had only days left to live and went out hell-raising for an entire six months before sinking into curious obscurity and then he had the neck to say to her, '*You* did that to me!'

Louse! Not the guy she recalled, but then there was no denying that she had had a very rosy and false image of Rocco until reality had smacked her in the teeth. That first night they'd met they had stayed up talking until way past dawn in a variety of public places. Her brain had been in a tailspin. She had let him take her home for breakfast and he had seduced her into bed with him. Well, possibly, she had been fairly willing to be seduced for the first time in her cautious existence. After all, she had only been in love once before Rocco and that had been nothing but a great big let-down.

She grimaced, recalling Russ, whom she had fallen for the year before she'd met Rocco. Meeting Opal over dinner one evening, Russ had taken one stunned look at her beautiful sister and had barely noticed Amber's existence from that point on. Sitting there like a third wheel while the man she'd thought she'd loved had ignored her and flirted like mad with her sister, Amber had stopped thinking he was special. That very night, Amber had been planning to surrender to Russ's persuasions and acquire her first experience of making love. But by the time Russ had finished raving about how gorgeous and how totally fabulous and fascinating Opal was, Amber had known she never, ever wanted to see him again. Opal turned heads in the street with her flawless ice-blonde perfection. As Amber had learned to her cost, a lot of men couldn't handle that.

Rocco had never got the chance to make the same mistake.

Their first day together, Rocco had woken Amber up

about lunchtime and told her that he had been looking for someone like her *all* his life. Well, all his life from the night before, she could only assume in retrospect. Rocco, who had stood outside his own locked bathroom door swearing that it was *so* romantic that she had fallen into his bed within hours of meeting him, declaring that he did not have one-night stands, that he would never, ever *think* of her in that light and finally, in desperation, apologising for not having kept his far-too-persuasive hands off her. On the other side of the door, she had been biting back sobs of chagrined self-loathing and struggling into her clothes with frantic hands.

'I'm not letting you go,' Rocco told her when she emerged. 'I'm hanging onto you.'

Three months of excitement and joy, interspersed with occasional violent rows that tore her apart at the seams, followed. No longer did she want to work endless overtime: she wanted to be with Rocco but she valued her career. Rocco offered her a position on his own staff at much more than she was earning. She didn't speak to him for two solid days. Such a casual proposition insulted all that she had achieved on her own merits. Rocco had made the very great error of allowing her to see how unimportant and small that job of hers was on his terms.

Crazy about him, she stopped having lunch and taking breaks at work and socialised equally crazy hours, burning the candle at both ends. She fell asleep on him once over dinner in a busy restaurant.

'Such a compliment,' Rocco quipped.

When she appeared in photos by Rocco's side in the gossip columns, she began receiving pointed cracks and knowing looks from her male co-workers. One of the directors provoked a chorus of sniggers the day he thanked her for giving Woodlawn Wyatt so much free publicity. Her working environment was one where men lived in eager hope of seeing a manipulative woman using her body to get ahead. Having an affair with a wealthy and powerful international financier was not the ticket to earning respect.

'Why won't you give me the chance to meet Rocco?' Opal demanded of Amber repeatedly. 'A quick drink early some evening…an hour, no big deal, Amber.'

Amber viewed her sibling's pure, perfect face and her heart sunk for she knew she could not compete. Not in looks, not in wit, not in *any* field. 'It's not cool to confront guys with your family. It might give him the wrong message—'

'You're very insecure about him. I suppose you can't believe your good luck in attracting a male of his calibre and are still wondering what he sees in you,' Opal remarked with deadly accuracy. 'But if he's a commitment-phobe, better to find out now than later. Don't do what I once did. Don't waste five years of your life making excuses for him and chasing rainbows.'

And that was the surprising moment when Amber learned that her sister, whom she had naively assumed to be ultra-successful in *every* way, disabused her of that notion. Prior to meeting Neville, Opal had apparently been strung along by an older man she'd adored and then been ditched when she'd least expected it. That confession of vulnerability allowed Amber to feel close to her older sister for the first time. But the one person she could have trusted with her confidences, she refused to trust.

By the time she had been with Rocco an entire three months, Amber was literally bursting with the simple human need to verbally share her happiness with someone. It was sheer deprivation to have no friend in whom to confide the news that Rocco was the most romantic, the most wonderful guy in the world. Years of attending evening classes several nights a week and working long hours had left Amber without close friends. Dinah Fletcher had gone to school with Amber, made the effort to get Amber's phone number from Opal and rang up out of the blue to suggest a girly get-together, a catching-up on old times…

Deep in her disturbing memories of that disastrous evening with Dinah, Amber hoisted herself up onto the low, sturdy branch of a giant conifer and braced her spine against the trunk. At least everything was still dry below the thick tree canopy, she reflected ruefully, staring up at the loose dead branch pointed out to her by her employer and wondering how best to dislodge it. Reaching down for the leaf rake, she clambered awkwardly higher.

Hearing the rustling, noisy passage of something moving at speed through the undergrowth, she stiffened in dismay, recalling her experience of being cornered by a very aggressive dog a few weeks back. The owner, a guest of the Wintons', had called the animal off, boasting about what a great guard dog he was, not seeming to care that Amber had been scared witless. But now when she peered down anxiously from her perch, she saw that it was Rocco powering like an Olympic sprinter into the clearing below. Her tension ironically increased.

'What the hell are you trying to do to yourself?' Rocco roared at her from twenty feet away. 'Get down from there!'

Amber assumed that now that the rain had quit he was the advance guard of a larger party getting the official tour of the woods, and her teeth gritted in receipt of that interfering demand. 'Why are you trying to make me look like a clown when I'm only trying to do my job?' she snapped in a meaningful whisper. 'Do you think I'm up here for fun?'

Lean, bronzed features stamped with furious exasperation, Rocco strode up to the tree, removed the leaf rake dangling from her loosened grasp and pitched it aside. 'If you knock that hanging branch down, it's going to smash your head in!'

'I'm as safe as houses standing here!'

'Don't be bloody stupid!' Rocco reached up and simply snatched her bodily off her perch. As he did so, the branch on which she'd stood bounced and sent a shiver up through the tree. With a creaking noise, the loose branch above them lurched free of its resting place and began to crash down.

Rocco moved fast, but not fast enough to retain his balance when he was carrying her. Sliding on the soft carpet of leaves below the trees, he went down with her on top of him. Weak with relief that neither of them had been hurt, Amber kept her face buried in his shirt-front, drinking in the achingly familiar scent of him that clung to the fibres, listening to the solid thump of his heartbeat.

'So how are you planning to say thank you?' Rocco enquired lazily.

Amber pushed herself up on forceful hands and scrambled backwards and off him as if she had been burnt. 'Thank you? When you almost killed both of us?'

'I saved your life, woman.' Raw self-assurance charging every syllable of that confident declaration, Rocco strode over to survey the smashed pieces of wood strewing the ground. 'Winton should have hired a forester or a tree surgeon for this kind of work—'

'He's too mean to pay their rates.' Her uncertain gaze followed him and stayed with him. In a dark green weatherproof jacket, his well-worn denim jeans accentuating his lean hips and long, powerful thighs, the breeze ruffling his luxuriant silver fair hair above his lean, dark, devastating features, Rocco looked so sensational, he just took her breath away. 'How come you seem to be out here on your own?'

'I'm escaping some *serious* Monopoly players.' Rocco leant back with fluid grace against the tree trunk and surveyed her with heavily lidded eyes, his gaze a golden gleam below dense, dark lashes.

'Monopoly? You're kidding me?' Amber said unevenly, wandering skittishly closer, then beginning to edge away again as she registered what she was doing.

'I'm not into board games.' He stretched out his long arms and captured her by the shoulders before she could move out of reach. 'You're pale…all shaken up.'

'Maybe…' Amber connected with his stunning dark golden eyes and she wanted to say something smart, but all inventiveness failed her.

Rocco tugged her to him with easy strength. 'I'll be gone in a couple of hours.'

'Gone?' In the act of forcing herself to pull back from him, Amber stilled in shock. She wasn't prepared for that shock, either. Indeed the shock came out of nowhere at her like a body blow. He was a weekend guest, *of course* he was leaving. 'But it's only Saturday,' she heard herself muttering weakly.

'Twenty-four hours of the Wintons goes a long way, tabbycat.' Framing her taut cheekbones with long, sure fingers, Rocco extracted a hungry, drugging kiss as if it were the most natural thing in the world.

Amber was defenceless, all concentration already shot by the knowledge of his imminent departure. Leaning into him, she slid her hands beneath his jacket to rest against his crisp cotton shirt. Shivering, desperate hunger had her in a stranglehold. Going, going, gone… I can't *bear* it, screamed a voice inside her head. Her heartbeat racing at an insane rate beneath the onslaught of that skilful kiss, she blocked out that voice she didn't want to hear.

'While one minute of you doesn't last half long enough,' Rocco husked, and let his tongue pry between her readily parted lips, once, twice, the third time making her shiver as though she were in a force-ten gale.

He stopped teasing and devoured her mouth with plundering force. She pulled his shirt out of his waistband, allowed her seeking fingers to splay against the warm smooth skin of his waist, felt him jerk in response. He dragged her hand down to the hard, thrusting evidence of his very male arousal. Her fingertips met the rough, frustrating barrier of denim. He pushed against her with a muffled groan of frustration, angled his head back from her, feverish golden eyes glittering, to say with ragged mockery, 'No sheet to hide under out here, *cara*.'

'Rocco…' Cheeks flaming, she was assailed by bittersweet memories that hurt even as they made her shiver and melt down deep inside where she ached for him. And the combination released a flood of recklessness. She stretched up and claimed his sensual mouth again for herself and jerked at his belt with trembling fingers. He tensed in surprise against her and then suddenly he was coming to her assistance faster than the speed of light, releasing the buttons on his tight jeans.

The feel of Rocco trembling like a stallion at the starting gate was the most powerful aphrodisiac Amber had ever experienced. Her own legs barely capable of holding her up, she slid dizzily down his hard, muscular physique onto her knees.

She pressed her lips into his hard, flat stomach and then sent the tip of her tongue skimming along the line of his loosened waistband. His muscles jerked satisfyingly taut under that provocative approach and he exhaled audibly. 'Don't tease…' he begged her, Italian accent thickening every urgent syllable. 'I couldn't stand it…'

'Stop trying to take control…' Taking her time, she ran her hands up his taut, splayed thighs, loving every gorgeous inch of him, loving the way just touching him made her feel. As she eased away the denim, dispensed with the last barrier, Rocco was shaking, breathing heavily. Finding the virile proof of his excitement was not a problem. The extraordinary effect she was having on him was turning her so hot and quivery inside, she was sinking deeper and deeper into a sensual daze.

As she took him in her mouth, he groaned her name out loud, arching his hips off the trunk in surging eagerness. She felt like every woman born since Eve; she felt a power she had never dreamt she could feel. He was *hers* and he was out of control as she had never known him to be. It gave her extreme pleasure to torture him. He meshed his hand into her hair, urging her on, and then he cried out in Italian and he shuddered into an explosive release when she chose, not when he chose.

In the aftermath, the birdsong came back to charge a silence that still echoed in her sensitive ears. She was so shaken up, her body so weak, she felt limp.

Rocco hauled her up to him to study her with dazed and wondering dark golden eyes and then he wrapped his arms round her, pulled her close, burying his face in her hair. He held her so tightly she could not fill her lungs with oxygen, but she revelled in that natural warmth and affection of his, which she had missed infinitely more than she had missed him in her bed. He muttered with a roughened laugh, 'Só…I sack the gardener at my own country estate. I hire you…I get into rustic daily walks…no problem, *cara*!'

Amber went rigid and, planting her hands against his broad chest, she pulled free of him like a bristling cat.

'Joke…' Rocco breathed when he saw her furiously flushed face. 'Obviously the wrong one.'

Amber wasn't so sure: Rocco had a very high sex drive. Rocco was still surveying her with stunned appreciation. Rocco always just reached out and took what he wanted. But she wasn't available; she wasn't on offer and never would be again.

'No encore. Goodbye, Rocco.'

'So you weren't in a joking mood—'

Amber crammed her shaking, restive hands into the pockets of her jacket as she backed away from him. 'Your days of being stalked by me are over…OK?'

'I openly admit that I was stalking *you* today, *cara*.'

'Do you think I didn't work that out for myself?' She forced a jarring laugh for she was actually only making that possible connection as he admitted it. 'But I turned the tables—'

'Yes. You also turned *me* inside out…' Rocco rested his intense golden eyes on her, a male well aware of the strength of his own powerful sexual appeal.

Amber dealt him a frozen look of scorn that took every ounce of her acting ability. 'So now you know how that feels.'

CHAPTER FIVE

THE instant Amber believed she was out of sight and hearing, she broke into a run, her breath rasping in her throat in a mad flight through the trees.

It was only four but it was getting dark fast. As Neville had promised, he had had her car brought back. She blundered past it into the cottage, shedding her jacket in a heap, pausing only to wrench off her boots. Not even bothering to put on the lights, she was heading up the stairs when she noticed the red light flashing on the answering machine. With a sigh, she hit the button in case it was something urgent.

Opal's beautifully modulated speaking voice filled the room. Opal and Neville had gone to visit friends, were staying on there for dinner with the children and were planning on a late return. 'Freddy's getting loads of attention,' her sister asserted. 'He won't get the chance to miss you. I'll put him to bed for you when we get back home.'

The prospect of hugging Freddy like a comforting security blanket that evening receded fast. Eyes watering, Amber hurried on upstairs. In the tiny shower room, she switched on the shower and pulled off her clothes as if she were in a race to the finish line. Stepping into the cubicle, she sent the door flying shut and stood there trembling, letting the warm water flood down over her.

What had got into her with Rocco? Sudden insanity? She didn't know what was happening inside her head any more and she was too afraid to take a closer look. All she remembered was feeling as if she were dying inside when Rocco had said he was leaving. So had she somehow had a brainstorm and imagined he was going to move in with the Wintons for ever? Rocco playing board games? Rocco, who was so full of restive, seething energy you could get tired watching him?

She sank down in the corner of the shower, letting the water continue to cascade down over her still-shivering body. What had come over her out in the woods? She didn't want to know. He was gone, he was history…he was *gone*. A horrendous mix of conflicting feelings attacked her. Rage…fear…pain. She hugged her knees and bowed her head down on them.

Rocco had come in search of her. He had admitted that. To say goodbye? Impossible to imagine the Rocco she remembered planning to take advantage of her smallest show of weakness and drag her down into the undergrowth to make love to her again. She would have said no anyway, she *definitely* would have said no, she told herself. He hadn't laid a finger on her, she reminded herself with equal urgency. But then, bombarded by erotic imagery which reminded her precisely why Rocco had been so unusually restrained, she uttered a strangled moan of shame. Rocco not having touched *her* was no longer a source of reassurance or comfort.

She hated him, she really did. She was over him, over him. She hadn't even been kissed in eighteen months, had conceived a violent antipathy for every male her brother-in-law had brought home to dinner in the hope she would take the bait and start dating again. Maybe that had something to do with how she had behaved with Rocco. Or maybe she just loved his body. *Yes.* Wanton, shameless…starved of him? *No*, she swore vehemently to herself. Just a case of over-charged emotions, confusion and an overdose of hormones out of sync. She stayed in the shower until the water ran cold.

Wrapping herself in a towel, she padded out of the shower room. She frowned at the sight of the dim light spilling from her bedroom out onto the landing. She hadn't even been in her bedroom yet. Had she left the bedside lamp switched on all day? If so, why hadn't she noticed it when she'd come upstairs earlier? Acknowledging that she had been in no state to notice anything very much and that she still felt hollow and sick inside, Amber pushed the door wider and walked into her room.

On the threshold, she froze. Rocco was poised by the window.

'How on earth—?'

'You didn't hear me knock and your front door was unlocked—'

'Was that an invitation for you to just walk on in?' Amber snapped, thinking how very lucky she was that he had not gone into Freddy's little room next door to hers first. Had he done so, he would hardly have failed to notice the cot and the toys in there.

He had changed out of his designer casuals. Sheathed in a formal dark business suit, his arrogant head within inches of the ceiling, Rocco looked for-midable.

Agitated by the severe disadvantage of having a scrubbed bare face, dripping hair in a tangle and only an old beach towel between herself and total nudity, Amber added, 'And walk right up into my bedroom?'

Rocco gave her a cloaked look. 'Since I've already said my goodbyes to my host, I didn't think you'd want me to advertise my presence by waiting downstairs in a room that doesn't even have curtains on the windows.'

Amber flushed at that accurate assumption. 'I haven't got around to putting any up yet,' she said defensively.

'I think a woman living alone and secluded by a big empty courtyard should be more careful of her own privacy and safety—'

Amber lifted her chin. 'You're the only prowling predator I've ever known. So what are you doing here?'

'When you turn me inside out, you take the consequences,' Rocco murmured with indolent cool.

'What's that supposed to mean?'

'That what you start, you have to finish.'

'We *are* finished,' she said breathlessly.

'I'm not hearing you…' Rocco sidestepped her and pushed the bedroom door closed like a guy making a pronounced statement.

'Rocco—'

'You want me…I want you. Right now, when I'm flying out to Italy for three days, everything else is superfluous.'

A tide of colour washed up over her heart-shaped face.

The expectant silence rushed and surged around her.

'Unless you say otherwise, of course,' Rocco spelt out with soft sibilance. 'I can't say goodbye to you again.'

Rocco wanted her back. She couldn't believe it. He had wrongfooted her, sprung a sneak attack, thrown her in a loop. She had had no expectations of him at all. She had said goodbye and she had meant it. But her saying goodbye had been kind of pointless when no other option had been on offer, an empty phrase that nonetheless could rip the heart out of her if she thought about it.

'You have incredible nerve…' she mumbled shakily, wondering what had happened to all that stuff about him never being able to trust her again, fighting to focus her brain on that mystery, utterly failing.

'No, I'm a ruthless opportunist.'

She saw that, could hardly miss that. Show weakness and Rocco took advantage. He had taught her that within twelve hours of their very first meeting. A brilliant, ruthless risk-taker whom she had once adored and could probably adore again, but the prospect terrified her. Freddy…what about her son, *their* son, Freddy? He didn't know about Freddy and she didn't think that it was quite the right moment to make that shock announcement. Rocco seemed to believe that the clock could be turned back and, dear heaven, she wanted to believe that too, *but*… A baby made a difference; Freddy *would* make a difference.

'So…' Rocco was studying her as she imagined he would study an opponent in the boardroom. With a cool, incisive intensity that sought to read the thoughts on her face. 'Do I go…or do I stay?'

No, it really wasn't the moment to ask him how he felt about being a father and, since it was his fault she had fallen pregnant in the first place, he was really just going to have to come to terms with Freddy. Oh, yes, Rocco, she thought with helpless tender amusement, unlike you once assured me, it *is* that easy to get pregnant. He might reign supreme in every other corner of his organised, fast-moving existence, but fate had had the last laugh in the field of conception.

'You've got a big smile in your beautiful eyes,' Rocco drawled with a wolfish grin that twisted her vulnerable heart.

He jerked loose his silk tie.

'You could be taking a lot for granted,' she said, trying to play it cool.

'I took you for granted until I had to get by without you. When I saw you last night, I became a very fast learner,' Rocco asserted, shimmying his wide shoulders back with easy grace and casting off his superb tailored suit jacket.

'No servants here, Rocco... I'm not picking up after you,' Amber whispered, heart hurling itself against her ribcage, making her feel dizzy.

Rocco vented a rueful laugh. 'So I'm not tidy.'

It had been so long since she'd heard him laugh like that, she wanted to tape him; she wanted to capture the moment, stop time dead, just look, listen, rejoice. She picked up his jacket; she couldn't help it. She couldn't bear to see expensive clothes treated like rags of no account. She hugged his jacket to her, happiness beginning to soar like a bird taking flight inside her. Thank you, God, she chanted with silent fervour, thank you.

As far as she was concerned, Rocco's slate of sins was wiped clean. Within the space of twenty-four hours, Rocco had transformed himself from being a stubborn, angry, unforgiving louse full of wild allegations back into the charismatic lover she had lost. Hadn't he just said that he had taken her for granted until he had had to get by without her? Had he been too proud to seek her out after his anger had ebbed?

He flung his shirt on the chair where she was draping his jacket. She gave him a sunny smile of approval. 'Did you drive yourself down here? Where's your car?' she asked.

'Parked in the back lane...this is like having an illicit assignation.'

She tensed. 'And how much do you know about that?'

'I don't mess around with married women.'

At that grounding admission, a little of her buoyancy ebbed. 'But you haven't exactly spent the past eighteen months *pining*...let's be frank.'

Stilling, Rocco sent her a slanting glance of scorching hunger.

She was vaguely surprised that her towel didn't go up in flames, but the pain she was suppressing wouldn't let go of her. 'Stop evading the issue...'

A faint rise of dark blood accentuated his fabulous high cheekbones. His equally fabulous mouth tautened. 'I was on the rebound...I was trying to replace you. I don't want to talk about that,' he completed with brooding abruptness, lush black lashes lifting, stormy golden eyes challenging her.

Was that guilt or regret she was hearing? Or back off, mind your own business? Amber turned away. A split second later, he was behind her, tugging her back against him with possessive hands. 'So how many other men have there been?' he said in the same tone he might have utilised to read a weather report, but his big powerful frame was so tense it betrayed him.

'Back off...mind your own business,' Amber heard herself say.

'*But—*'

'I don't want to talk about it.' She flung back the same words he had given her.

'Sooner or later you'll tell me,' Rocco forecast, and swept her right off her feet in a startling demonstration of his superior strength to carry her over to her own bed. 'You tell me *everything*.'

'Not quite everything...no one tells everything.'

He settled her down on the bed and then lifted her again to yank the duvet from beneath her. He came down beside her, like a vibrant bronze image of raw masculinity, and detached the tuck on her towel with long brown fingers. Smouldering tawny eyes scanned her hectically flushed face. 'I'll get it out of you, tabbycat.'

She lifted an unsteady hand to trace the course of one hard, angular cheekbone. 'Don't call me that unless you mean it,' she whispered helplessly. 'I don't want you hurting me again.'

He caught her fingers and kissed them, ridiculously long inky lashes screening his gaze from her. 'I would never set out to hurt you and I never say anything I don't mean.'

In receipt of those assurances, her attack of insecurity ebbed, but she was already very conscious of her own intense vulnerability. She had got by without Rocco by persuading herself that she hated him. Now the scary truth was blinding her. She was still crazy about him. Her barriers were down. Putting them back up would be impossible for her a second time.

CHAPTER SIX

'YOU'RE so serious, *cara*,' Rocco censured huskily.

And tonight, 'serious' was obviously not what was required, Amber interpreted without much difficulty. That *wasn't* like him, she thought uneasily, but she suppressed that suspicion and concentrated instead on being seriously happy.

'Smile…' Rocco urged, tumbling her back into the pillows and arranging himself over her, so that not one inch of her was bare of his potent presence.

Amber smiled brighter than the sun because she was with him again. He kissed her in reward. She even tried to smile under his marauding mouth and her heart sang, her senses flowering to the taste and the touch and the scent of him again. Every fibre of her being was on a knife edge of delicious anticipation.

He found her breasts with a husky sound in the back of his throat that was incredibly sexy. Her sensitised flesh swelled into his shaping palms and she trembled in response. He rested appreciative eyes on the full, pouting mounds. 'I swear that though the rest of you has got thinner, your gorgeous breasts…*per amor di Dio*— just looking at you makes me ache,' he ground out with thickened fervour. 'You're every erotic dream I have ever had, *cara*.'

Amber was aware that pregnancy *had* changed her shape. She tensed, but Rocco chose that exact same moment to give way to temptation and send his dark head swooping down to capture a throbbing pink nipple in his mouth. Her ability to think was wrenched from her at speed. Her eyes squeezed tight shut and her spine arched. As he teased at the stiff, tender buds begging for his attention, nothing existed for her for long, timeless moments but the all-encompassing surge of her own writhing response. She had always been intensely sensitive there. Pulsing waves of intense pleasure cascaded through her quivering body as she yielded to his erotic mastery.

'I *missed* you so much…' she gasped, mouth dry, throat tight, breathing a challenge.

He reclaimed her reddened lips with fierce, plundering passion, his hands knotting into her damp honey-blonde hair, lifting her to him as if he could never get enough of her. His tongue delved deep into her mouth and her thighs clenched together on a need that already felt shockingly intolerable. He kissed her until she was moaning and clinging to him and he only paused to catch his own breath.

He studied her passion-glazed eyes with intense male satisfaction. 'When I saw you getting out of that car this morning, I felt violent,' he declared with raw force as he shifted with innate eroticism against her, acquainting her with the bold, hot proof of his hard arousal. 'I wanted to rip that guy out of his Merc and beat him to a pulp. Then I wanted to drag you off like a caveman and imprint myself so deeply on you that you would never look at another man again!'

'Neville's my brother-in-law,' Amber reminded him, aghast.

'They can't *all* have been relatives—'

As Rocco loomed over her, all domineering male,

Amber ran worshipping hands up over his magnificent hair-roughened torso, adoring the hard strength and beauty of him, and he shivered, rippling muscles pulling taut. But shimmering stubborn golden eyes still gazed down into hers. 'I only want a number...I've no wish to talk about them—'

'No...someone as possessive as you are doesn't want a number either,' Amber whispered, a rueful giggle tugging at her vocal cords, even as his hand tightened on her hip and dragged her closer and her wanton body turned liquid as heated honey.

'Ballpark figure?' he pressed with roughened determination.

Amber exerted pressure on his big brown shoulders to tug him back to her again. It would be so easy to admit that there had never been anyone else, but the mean streak in her wouldn't let her tell him that yet. If, and when, he deserved that honesty.

'*Dio mio*...it's driving me crazy thinking about you with other—'

'Shush...' Amber came up on one elbow and pressed her tingling mouth to his again.

Rocco went rigid and then he vented a hungry groan and he responded with devastating, driving sensuality. She laced her fingers into his thick, tousled hair, weak and quivering with a hunger as unstoppable as a flood-tide. Every time her sensitised skin came into glancing contact with any part of his lean, hard frame, the heat building inside her and the tormenting ache for fulfilment increased.

'Rocco...' she moaned as he thumbed the aching buds of her breasts and lingered there, giving her ruthless pleasure with indolent ease.

Skimming sure fingers through the silky fleece of curls at the junction of her thighs, he pressed his carnal mouth to the tiny pulse flickering at her collarbone, making every skin-cell leap. Her blood started roaring through her veins, her heart thundering in her own ears. As he explored the hot, damp welcome awaiting him, she could not stay still and all control was taken from her. There was only Rocco and what he was doing to her with such exquisite expertise, the burning need that sent her hips rising from the bed, the choked sounds wrenched from her with ever greater frequency.

'Please…' she sobbed.

He pulled her under him, spread her thighs with an urgency that betrayed his own urgent need. She collided with feverish golden eyes and a great wave of love infused her.

'I never thought I would *be* with you again…' Rocco groaned with raw, feeling intensity as he tipped her up and drove deep into her moist satin sheath.

She arched up to receive him, a stunned cry of response torn from her for she had forgotten just how incredible he could make her feel, forgotten that bold sensation of being stretched to accommodate him. He set a pagan rhythm and with every fluid thrust he excited her beyond bearing. Every hot, abandoned inch of her revelled in his strength and masculine dominance. His passionate force drove her wild with excitement until at last he allowed her to surge over the final threshold. That shattering climax felt endless to her, splintering through her writhing body in long, ecstatic waves of release. Utterly lost in him, mindless with delight, she whimpered and clung as he shuddered over her and slammed into her one last time with a harsh groan of very male pleasure.

'Nobody can make me feel like you do, tabbycat…' Rocco vented an indolent sigh of satisfaction. Smoothing her hair from her brow, he stole a tender, lingering kiss from her swollen lips and hugged her close.

She kissed his shoulder, drowning in the hot, damp smell of his skin, loving him. It felt like coming home. She could not credit that he had only come back into her life the night before, for it now felt to her as though they had never been apart…as though the whole dreadful nightmare of that cheap and sleazy spread in a down-market newspaper had never happened. 'When did you start appreciating that I must have been set up by Dinah Fletcher?' she murmured curiously.

His big, powerful frame tensed. Lifting his tousled fair head, he rested dark as midnight eyes on her, superb bronzed bone-structure taut. He was still in her arms but she recognised his instantaneous withdrawal by the impassivity of his gaze. It was as if he had slammed a door in her face. 'We haven't got time to talk. I have to be out of here in fifteen minutes.'

As Rocco rolled free of her and sprang out of bed, Amber was stunned. 'You have to be out of here in fifteen *minutes*?'

'What began as an excuse to extract me from this weekend early turned into the real McCoy,' Rocco quipped on his way out of the room. 'I have to work out a rescue package for a hotel chain which belongs to friends of mine by Tuesday.'

Obviously he had known that before he'd come to see her. She just wished he had mentioned how little time he had to spend with her. On the one hand, she felt hurt and disappointed, but she was also aware that Rocco's talents were always very much in demand. It was also exactly like him to drop everything to go to the assistance of a friend. She listened to the shower running, knew he would find very little, if any, hot water.

'I'm not a fan of primitive plumbing, *cara*,' Rocco commented with a feeling shudder on his return to the bedroom. 'I'll organise a car to move you out of here tomorrow.'

'Move me *out*...of here?' Amber prompted unevenly, immediately wondering if he was asking her to live with him and wondering how she would answer him if that was what he meant. Everything felt as if it was happening way too fast for common sense, but it had always been like that with Rocco.

Rocco dropped the towel wrapped round his lean brown hips. Attention straying, she swallowed hard. He was magnificent: the lean, muscular power of a very fit male laced with the overwhelming appeal of a very sexual animal. Her cheeks burned. He was drop-dead gorgeous but gaping at him made her feel embarrassed for herself in spite of the renewed intimacy between them.

'I *have* to come clean with you,' Rocco murmured with rueful emphasis. 'I'm afraid I overreacted when I first realised you were working for the Wintons yesterday...'

Amber nodded agreement, glad he was admitting that reality.

His expressive mouth tightened and then he breathed in deep. 'But by the time you came indoors to reason with me, I had *already* called Harris and warned him that you might only be marking time here in search of a story worth selling.'

Amber turned pale with horror at that most belated confession.

'I'm sorry.' Rocco spoiled his seemingly sincere apology, however, by adding, 'But it's not really a problem now, is it?'

'What did Mr Winton say?' Amber demanded tensely, only now recalling how cool the older man had been with her earlier in the day, but she hadn't even suspected that there might have been anything personal in his apparent preoccupation.

'He'll be looking for grounds to sack you and get you off his property as fast as possible.' Rocco followed that devastating assurance with a shrug of incredible cool. 'But since this is not a convenient neck of the woods for you to live when I'm based in London when I am in the UK, it hardly matters—'

'It hardly matters…' Amber parroted in a shattered tone of disbelief. 'You tell me that you've virtually got me the sack and that I'm likely to be kicked out of this cottage…and you *think* that's no big deal?'

Rocco elevated a dark, imperious brow. 'Like you really love that wheelbarrow and living in this dump!' he derided.

'I won't even dignify that with an answer!' she said in reproach, appalled by his seeming indifference to the plight he had put her in.

His white shirt hanging open on his bronzed, hair-roughened chest, Rocco strolled over to the bed and crouched down to her level. Tawny eyes rested on her shaken and furious face. He closed his big hands over hers, strenuously ignoring her attempt to pull free of his grasp. 'It goes without saying that, from this moment on, I will take care of *all* your expenses so you really do have nothing at all to worry about.'

She stared back at him in astonishment.

Rocco released his hold on her and lifted lean brown fingers to brush her hair back from one taut cheekbone in a soothing, but nonetheless very confident, gesture of intimacy. 'It's the only thing that makes sense and you know it—'

Pale as death, Amber compressed bloodless lips, but she couldn't stop herself trembling. 'You never brought money into our relationship before—'

His lean, powerful face clenched. 'It was a different relationship.'

'Different?' Amber echoed and she could hear her own voice fading away on her, for this terrible fear was building inside her that she had entirely misunderstood what he had meant by coming back to her.

In an abrupt movement, Rocco vaulted back upright again.

The silence stretched into infinity.

'Explain that word "different" to me,' Amber whispered tightly.

'It would be hard to quantify it.'

'Oh, I think I can quantify it *for* you,' Amber muttered in an agony of humiliation, but she didn't speak her thoughts aloud. She had given him sex and he had come back for more sex and the foreseeable future would include only very much more of the same. Being a wanton in the woods had rebounded on her. He thought he could have her back on any terms now.

'We can't pretend the past never happened. Naturally things have changed. But there's nothing wrong with my wish to look after you.'

'Look after me…with a view to what in the future?' Amber asked shakily.

Rocco chose that exact moment to turn his back to her searching eyes and duck down low enough to use the dressing mirror and straighten his tie. 'Whatever happens, I'll be there for you. I don't turn my back on my responsibilities. You're making a fuss about nothing.'

Amber was so crushed she couldn't think straight. She was thinking of Freddy: Freddy who was very much Rocco's responsibility. Somehow Amber did not think that Rocco would be quite so keen to reacquire a lover who had already given birth to his child.

'I won't be your mistress, your kept woman, whatever you want to call it,' she stated curtly. 'I thought you cared about me—'

'*Santo Cielo*…of course, I care about you! Stop dramatising the situation,' Rocco whipped back round to rest his stunning dark gaze on her in cool challenge. 'Be practical. Right now you're as poor as a church mouse!'

Amber lost even more colour and studied her tightly linked hands.

'No doubt if I was as poor as a church mouse and on the brink of being unemployed and homeless as well, *you* would offer to keep *me*!' Rocco continued in a very specious argument, attempting to present the unacceptable in an acceptable guise.

'You would starve sooner than take me up on the offer. Furthermore,' she countered tightly, 'you dug yourself into a hole when you phoned Harris Winton and screwed up my job security, so you can hardly walk away *without* having me on your conscience—'

'Couldn't I?' Rocco shot her an exasperated appraisal. 'I could have just handed you a cheque in compensation. Are you coming to London or not?'

She swallowed the thickness in her throat. *'No…'*

Rocco withdrew a gold pen from his jacket. 'I'll leave my phone number with you—'

'No…'

'I'm not about to grovel,' Rocco grated.

'You're refusing even to discuss that newspaper story last year!' Amber condemned.

'If we talk about it, I might just wring your neck!' Rocco sent her startled face a flashing look of censure. 'I did not appreciate being publicly labelled a five-times-a-night stud—'

'But I never *said* that…I didn't make one tiny mention of even sleeping with you!' Amber gasped strickenly.

'So how come it was true?' Rocco growled, unimpressed by that plea of innocence.

'Lucky guess?' she muttered chokily.

'The day after that trash was printed, I walked into a Mayfair restaurant with a client and a bunch of city traders at the next table stood up and gave me a slow handclap.' The banked-down rage in his stormy gaze at that unfortunate recollection flailed her.

Amber just cringed.

'But I could have got over that…it was the sense of betrayal I couldn't take,' Rocco spelt out fiercely. 'I trusted you. When you really care about someone, you're loyal and you don't discuss that person with anyone else!'

'If you still believe that I would've discussed our intimacy with anybody, then get out of here because I don't want you near me!' Amber told him feverishly, but she was horribly impressed by his definition of caring.

'If you can't take the heat, you should have stayed out of the kitchen, tabbycat,' Rocco responded with silken derision. 'Don't start thinking that giving me a great time in bed automatically wipes out what you did last year!'

Amber stood up on hollow legs. At that crack, an uneven laugh escaped her. 'I am *so* much more forgiving than you are—'

'What have *you* got to forgive?'

Just at that moment, Amber felt dead inside, as if he had killed all her feelings. 'You didn't love me enough. I can see that now…odd, how I refused to face that at the time. A man who *really* loved me would have given me the chance to explain myself.'

His darkly handsome features clenched, 'Amber—'

Amber turned away. 'Please leave—'

'I haven't got time for this right now,' Rocco delivered, his tone sufficient to tell her that he wasn't taking her seriously.

'So *go*!'

'You don't mean that.'

Amber breathed in so deep, she marvelled that she didn't explode and fizzle round the ceiling above him.

Rocco reached the door and spread fluid and confident hands. 'You'll be on the phone within twenty hours—'

Amber's teeth gritted together.

'You need me.'

'No, I needed you eighteen months ago,' Amber countered fiercely. 'But I *don't* need you now. I got by without you once and I will again. If I get in touch with you in the next few days, Rocco…I warn you, it won't be about *us*.'

Rocco sent her a sudden vibrant grin of amusement. 'I'll see you in London, tabbycat.'

Only if she went, she wouldn't be arriving alone, Amber thought heavily. She listened to the slam of the front door downstairs and hugged herself. He didn't listen; he *never* listened to what he didn't want to hear. It wasn't that he had a huge ego. No, Rocco had something much harder to deflate: immense and boundless confidence. In addition, he had once been tremendous at second-guessing her every move. Only this time, he was miscalculating because there was a factor he didn't know about. *I would never set out to hurt you.* Stinging tears burned her eyes. She felt even more alone than she had felt when she had finally appreciated that she was pregnant by a man who wouldn't even take a phone call from her. Why, oh, why had she been such a fool as to imagine that the clock could be turned back when Rocco had never loved her in the first place?

CHAPTER SEVEN

IT WAS ironic that Harris Winton could not conceal his dismay when Amber went up to the house and tendered her resignation without notice early the following morning.

'I'm not a media spy, Mr Winton, and I'm not leaving because I have some poison-pen article written either,' Amber declared with wry humour and, now that she was leaving, not caring what opinion she left in her wake, continued, 'Rocco gets a little carried away sometimes. I'm going because it no longer suits me to work here.'

After the turmoil of the night, a strange accepting calm settled over her as she drove over to her sister's house. It had been a pretty awful job and she hated being so dependent on Opal and Neville's charity and seeing so little of her son. Freddy was growing fast and he wouldn't be a baby for much longer. It was time to make fresh choices and leave pride and personal feelings out of the question. The guy who had sworn he didn't turn his back on his responsibilities was about to find out that he *had*. How he felt about that, she didn't much care at that moment.

Opal was rarely taken by surprise. Reclining on a sofa in her elegant drawing room, looking very much like a fairy-tale princess with her flowing pale blonde hair and her exquisite face, she smiled with satisfaction when Amber announced that she had given up on gardening. 'You can move back in here immediately. It was very convenient having you here as second in command with the children. It suited you too. You saw much more of Freddy.'

'Thanks, but I've decided to move back to London.' Amber drew in a deep breath as Opal's fine brows elevated. 'I'm going to tell Rocco about Freddy—'

Her sister sat up with a start. 'Are you crazy?'

Amber would have much preferred not to admit that Rocco had been staying with the Wintons earlier that weekend but in the circumstances it wasn't possible. As she completed her halting explanation about having 'got talking' with Rocco and certain fences having been partially mended, while refusing to indicate *which* fences, her sister wore her most cynical expression of freezing incredulity.

Opal then looked at her in outright disgust. 'So Rocco Volpe just snaps his fingers and you throw up everything and go running—'

'It's not like that—'

'Isn't it? You didn't *tell* him about Freddy and we both know why, don't we? But what was the point of keeping quiet? The guy will laugh in your face if you try and pin a kid on him!' Opal forecast.

Amber paled.

'You'll humiliate yourself for nothing. He'll walk out on you and if you hear one more word from him, I guarantee it will be through his lawyer!' Opal continued.

'Maybe…but I'm doing what I should have done a year ago,' Amber declared tightly. 'Not for my sake, but for Freddy's. I want the right to tell my son who his father is and not have anybody laugh in my face *or* his.'

'Tell me, are you imagining that Rocco will open his arms to your child and turn into Daddy of the Year?' Opal demanded with total derision.

Amber studied her sister with hurt, bewildered eyes. 'I don't have *any* expectations at all. I don't know how he's likely to react. But I thought you'd think I was doing the right thing.'

'You're making yet *another* big mistake.'

'I don't think so.' It took courage for Amber to stand up to her sister.

'Why don't you tell Amber the truth about why you feel the way you do, Opal?' Neville had appeared in the doorway, his frank blue eyes pinned to the wife he adored with rare disapproval.

'Stay out of this, Neville—'

'I'm sorry, I can't.' The older man sighed. 'You're too prejudiced. The man who let *you* down was a married man—'

Amber stilled at that revelation and looked at her sister in astonishment. 'The man you told me about, the commitment-phobe you were with for five years, was *married* to another woman?'

Twin highspots of furious colour now burned over Opal's cheekbones.

'And like most married men having an affair, he couldn't run far enough when your sister told him she was expecting his child,' Neville completed heavily.

'Is this true?' Amber questioned her rigid and silent sister. 'You were pregnant?'

'I miscarried…fortunately,' Opal admitted curtly. 'But those facts have no bearing on the advice I've given you.'

Amber could not have agreed with that appraisal. She had just seen in Opal's rigid face the depth of her sister's bitterness, her sister's own memory of humiliation and rejection at the hands of the married man she had loved. Naturally that experience had coloured the forceful opinions which Opal had given Amber. 'I'm sorry you got into a situation like that,' she said awkwardly. 'But I wish you had told me the whole story.'

Ten minutes later, Freddy crawling round her feet in pursuit of a wooden car, Amber called the number Rocco had left with her. She got an answering machine and all she could do was leave a message.

However, within an hour Rocco called her back. Having answered the phone, her still-frozen-faced sister extended the receiver to Amber as if it were an offensive weapon.

'When do you want to travel?' Rocco asked, disconcerting her with that prosaic opening question, for she had expected a variety of greetings and that had not been one of them.

'The day you're coming back,' she said stiltedly. 'But I'll drive myself up—'

'You sound terrified. You won't regret this,' Rocco swore huskily.

'I think you *will*,' Amber muttered tautly. 'I'm just warning you...OK?'

'When did I contrive to forget that you're a pessimist, who nourishes negative expectations of anything new and different?' Rocco loosed an extravagant sigh.

'You haven't even told me where we...' She stumbled in dismay. 'I mean, *I'm* going to stay—'

'No, that's why you have to be collected and you can't drive yourself. I very much want to surprise you—'

'I don't like surprises.'

'Within a week of Christmas, that is *not* good news, tabbycat.'

'Don't call me that,' Amber told him woodenly.

'Whatever you say,' Rocco drawled with scrupulous politeness. 'We'll cancel Christmas too, shall we? Obviously you're not in the mood for it either.'

'Look, I've got to go,' Amber muttered, blinking back hot tears and swallowing hard. 'I'll see you when you get back to London.'

CHAPTER EIGHT

Two days later, a long, opulent limousine drew up to collect Amber from her sister's home.

The uniformed chauffeur was somewhat disconcerted to be confronted with a disassembled cot, a baby seat, a buggy, two bulging suitcases and a laundry basket full of toys and other unavoidable essentials.

'Will you get it all in?' Amber asked anxiously.

'Of course, madam.'

Before leaving for work, Neville had pressed a mobile phone on her. 'I think you should've given Rocco fair warning of what's coming. I'll be working late at the car showroom tonight. If there's a problem, wherever you are just call me and I'll come and collect you and Freddy.'

Opal had been even blunter. 'Don't be surprised if Rocco takes one look at Freddy and slams the door in your face! I cannot credit that you are doing this. It's *insane*...it's like something a foolish teenager would do.'

Amber only began to question what she was doing and how she was doing it on the drive to London. That was when she recognised her own bitterness and her own seething desire and need to confront Rocco. It would have been more sensible to tell Rocco about Freddy without Freddy around. But then, in such circumstances, there really wasn't a right or an easy way, was there?

When the limo headed for Holland Park and turned beneath an imposing arched gateway and came to a halt in front of a picturesque Georgian mansion set within lush lawned grounds, Amber at first assumed it was a hotel. Realising that it was a private residence, she was taken aback. Was this where Rocco now lived? Eighteen months ago, he had been living in a penthouse apartment, opulent and impressive if not remotely cosy, the perfect backdrop for a single male.

An older woman greeted her, introducing herself as the housekeeper. Freddy was much admired. Rocco had been held up in Rome, Amber was informed, and was not expected back before nine that evening. As it sank in on Amber that Rocco had had her brought to his own home, her nervous tension began increasing. Of course, it didn't mean that he had plans for her to stay under the same roof for more than one night.

By eight, Freddy was tucked into his cot in a charming guest room and fast asleep after a more than usually active day. Almost an hour later, Amber heard a car pulling up outside. She was wearing a fitted burgundy skirt suit and high heels, her hair conditioned within an inch of its life to fall round her shoulders in shining waves. She wanted to knock him hard with what he had done to her life, but she definitely didn't want him looking at her and thinking that dumping her again would be no great sacrifice.

Rocco strode through the door of the drawing room as Amber reached it. She had only a single enervating glimpse of his startlingly handsome dark features before he hauled her into his arms, clamped her to his big, powerful frame and crushed her startled mouth beneath his with a groan of uninhibited hunger.

That passionate onslaught knocked her sideways. The taste of him after a three-day-long fast was too much altogether for her self-discipline. Every prepared speech just went out of her head and she clung to him to stay upright on knees that had turned weak. As he sent his tongue delving between her readily parted lips to search out the moist, tender interior in explicit imitation of a much more intimate invasion, Amber's temperature rocketed into outer space. Her whole body went into sensory overload in reaction, her breasts pushing against her bra, straining peaks pinching into taut, erect buds, a stirring desperate ache making her clench her trembling thighs together.

'It's a torment to stop and breathe, *cara*,' Rocco growled against her reddened mouth, gazing down at her with smouldering golden eyes. 'I just want to jump you like an animal. Three days can feel like half a lifetime, especially when I wasn't *sure* until the very last minute that you would come here.'

'Weren't you?' Blinking rapidly, Amber studied her clinging hands, which were pinned to his shoulders, and dragged them from him in an abrupt guilty motion, face burning.

'I would've driven down to fetch you if you had backed out on me. In any case, I ought to meet your sister and her husband,' Rocco stated without hesitation.

Amber stiffened and dropped her head at that unwelcome announcement. Why on earth did she have this terrible fear of Rocco meeting Opal? And then the answer she had long avoided out of her own reluctance to face it came to her. Opal would set out to charm and enchant and hog centre stage because Opal always did that with men. Neville's adoration alone wasn't enough to satisfy her sibling's ego.

'And right now,' Rocco continued as she focused on

him again, 'there is nothing I want to do more than carry you upstairs and make mad, passionate love to you *but*—'

'Rocco…' Amber was back on track again and striving to muster the words for her big announcement, and then she just blundered on into it before she lost any more momentum. 'When you ditched me, eighteen months back, I was *pregnant*!'

His black luxuriant lashes semi-screened his intent dark gaze, but his bone-structure had clenched hard. He stared at her with riveted attention. 'You can't have been—'

'I was actually two months pregnant by then, but I'm afraid I had no idea. I was losing weight, I wasn't eating properly or even sleeping enough, and my cycle had never been that regular. When we were still together, it didn't even occur to me that I might be pregnant because I never had the time to stop and think and worry,' Amber said in a driven rush. 'My life then was just one mad whirl.'

Rocco had been listening to her with an intensity as great as the stunned light growing in his dark as midnight gaze. 'Pregnant…'

It seemed to her that he could hardly bring himself to speak that word out loud and she could see for herself how appalled he was.

'But you were taking the contraceptive pill,' he continued hoarsely.

'I had only been taking it for a couple of weeks,' Amber reminded him uncomfortably. 'And if you cast your mind back—'

'I don't *need* to have my mind cast back,' Rocco interposed tautly, pacing over to the window to stare out at the street lights glowing behind the belt of trees surrounding the house, his wide back and powerful shoulders taut with strain beneath his tailored dove-grey suit jacket. 'You warned me that the doctor had said you needed to take extra precautions. It was the middle of the night and I had nothing left to use and *I* said that it wasn't that easy to get pregnant.'

Amber had certainly not expected such perfect recall of events.

'Famous last words,' Rocco conceded in a dark, roughened undertone. 'Famous *stupid* last words. Even as I spoke them I was wincing for myself, but I couldn't resist temptation long enough to do what I should have done. It was always like that with you, *bella mia*.'

'I could have said no,' Amber found herself pointing out in all fairness. 'But I didn't. I was irresponsible too.'

'I was your first lover and I'm seven years older and a lifetime more experienced,' Rocco countered harshly, swinging back to face her. He had turned a sort of ashen shade beneath his bronzed complexion and his strong facial bones were rigid. 'But after a few weeks had passed and you showed not the slightest sign of concern, I assumed we'd got away with our recklessness and I didn't think of the matter again.'

Amber flushed. 'I thought about the risk even less than you did.'

'It's not a risk I've ever taken with any other woman,' Rocco muttered heavily, his lean, strong hands clenching into fists and then slowly unclenching again as if he was willing himself into greater calm. 'So this is what changed in you, this is why you told me I might regret you coming here…everything is falling into place. *Porca miseria*…I have been incredibly slow on the uptake. Your bitterness and your anger were there for me to see. But there I was, believing like a plaster saint that only I was entitled to such feelings.'

'Rocco…'

Rocco lifted his hands and spread them in an almost aggressive silencing motion. 'I need a drink.'

He had already worked it all out, Amber registered. And although she had not expected him to react as if he had received the good news of a lifetime, she had equally well not been prepared for him to turn pale as death and head for the drinks cabinet.

'Do you want one?'

'No…'

'Neither do I.' With a hand that was noticeably unsteady, Rocco set the glass he had withdrawn back into the gleaming cabinet and thrust the door shut again as if he was warding off temptation. He settled sombre dark eyes on her. 'I'm afraid I don't know what to say to you—'

'You're speaking pretty loudly without saying very much.' Amber thought that his shock, horror and pallor gave her a fair enough indication of his feelings on finding out that he was a father. Certainly, a woman with a young child was no candidate for a free-wheeling affair and frequent foreign travel. But then she wasn't about to have an affair with him, she reminded herself urgently.

'Shock… I think I could have better stood this happening with anyone but you—'

As that statement sank in on Amber, the seemingly ultimate rejection, her tummy gave a sick somersault. 'How can you openly say that to me? *How?*'

'How *not*? Do you think I can simply shrug off what you've told me as if it never happened? Don't you think that just like you I'm going to be remembering this for the rest of my life?' Rocco demanded, more emotional than she had ever seen him.

Her brain fogging up in her efforts to understand what he was telling her, Amber gazed blankly back at him.

'Well, maybe *not* just like you,' Rocco adjusted, meeting her questioning eyes with frowning force. 'But surely taking such a decision was deeply upsetting?'

Amber had had just about enough of trying to follow a bewildering dialogue in which Rocco appeared to have lost his ability to put across clear meaning. 'Would you please pause for a moment and just tell me in plain English what you're talking about?'

'*What?* I was trying to be tactful. I didn't want to distress you,' Rocco ground out between clenched white teeth. 'But you don't seem to be that sensitive on the subject, do you? No, scratch that. I *didn't* say it…you *didn't* hear it. I swear I am not judging you. I wasn't there to offer support. I know that. I accept that—'

Amber tilted her honey-blonde head to one side and stared at him with very wide but no longer uncomprehending eyes. 'Tell me, is the word you're dancing all around but avoiding…abortion?'

Rocco went sort of sickly grey in front of her, a sheen of perspiration on his skin. He nodded jerkily and breathed in very deep.

'Did I accidentally speak that word without realising it?' Amber prompted on a rising note of incredulity.

Rocco shook his head in negative.

'So you just *assumed* that if I fell pregnant I would *naturally* rush off for a termination, did you?'

The silence sizzled like a live electric current.

His full attention welded to her, Rocco's brows pleated. 'Didn't you?'

'Didn't I?' Amber sucked in a vast amount of oxygen like a woman ready to enter a pitched battle with extreme aggression. 'No, I darned well didn't go off and have an abortion! You have got some *nerve* just arrogantly assuming that that's what I chose to do!'

'Right…right,' Rocco said again, evidently getting

his brain back into gear but not, it had to be said, at supersonic speed. 'You didn't have an abortion…you gave birth to our baby?'

He was recovering a more natural colour and straightening his shoulders again, Amber noted. Huge relief was emanating from him in perceptible waves. Amber was utterly transfixed and fascinated. She had never been able to read Rocco as easily as she did that moment.

'For that, I am very grateful,' Rocco asserted thickly at nowhere near his usual pace and making a visible effort to shake free of his shock. 'The other conclusion…it would have haunted my conscience for ever and we might never have come to terms with it. So, obviously, you gave our child up for adoption—'

'Excuse me?' Amber's temper was on a knife edge because she was so wound up.

'The thought of that breaks my heart too…' Rocco's dark, deep drawl shook slightly as he made that emotive admission.

'Really?' Amber was back to being fascinated and paralysed to the spot again.

'But it was very brave of you to go through the pregnancy and face that alone and a situation I will simply have to learn to live with,' Rocco framed like a guy picking every word while walking on ice likely to crack under him and drown him at any minute. 'I can…I will, but it is such a terrible loss for both of us, *bella mia*.'

'Yes, I suppose it would have been…at least, it would have been for me, certainly,' Amber heard herself mumbling. 'And I'm beginning to get the message that it would have been a terrible loss for you too. *So*—'

Rocco raised and spread fluidly expressive hands in an appeal for a pause in revelation. 'No more until I have had a drink. I am all shaken up.'

Amber watched him pour a brandy with a great deal less than his usual dexterity 'So you like children.'

'I think so…I haven't met many,' Rocco said hoarsely, carefully, and passed her a drink without being asked. 'But that time I thought I might have got you pregnant, I liked the idea.'

'Oh…did you?' Amber studied his clenched profile, recognised that he was still firing on really only one cylinder, and her heart overflowed. 'That's good, Rocco. Because, for what it's worth, your idea of what I would do when I found myself unexpectedly pregnant and without support is very badly off target.'

He focused on her with grave dark eyes, his strain palpable. 'How…off target?'

'Well, I didn't go for abortion and I didn't go for adoption. Oh, and before you make yet another wild deduction, I did not abandon my baby either or have him placed in foster care,' Amber informed him gently. 'In fact, my baby—*our* baby is upstairs right now…OK?'

The balloon glass dropped right out of Rocco's hand and fell soundlessly to the carpet. But it smashed noisily when he stood on it in his sudden surging step forward.

'If that is a joke, it's a lousy one,' he breathed raggedly.

Amber folded her arms. 'Unlike you, I don't crack jokes at the most inopportune moments. Freddy's upstairs sleeping in one of your guest rooms.'

Rocco gazed at her as if she had taken flight without wings before his eyes. He was totally stunned. 'Say that again…*Freddy*?'

'Your son, Freddy…I called him after my grandfather, who was about the only role model I wanted him to follow in my own family,' she said shakily.

'Upstairs…*here*?' Rocco shot at her incredulously, suddenly recovering his usual energy without warning. 'In my own home? I don't believe you!'

'You want to see him?'

Rocco wasn't waiting He was already striding out into the hall. Amber followed his forceful surge up the stairs. 'Room at the foot of the corridor… Rocco, if you wake him up before midnight, he'll scream blue murder. After midnight…even around two or three in the morning, he's bouncing about his cot and positively dying to socialise.'

'I'm not going to wake him up…OK?'

Amber insinuated herself between him and the door which had been left ajar. She pushed it wider. Light spilled in from the landing and, in concert with the nightlight Amber had brought with her, it shed a fair amount of clarity on the occupant of the cot. There Freddy lay in his all-in-one sleeper which was adorned with little racing car images.

Rocco mumbled something indecipherable in his own language and peered down into the cot, lean hands flexing and then bracing again on the side bars. Freddy shifted in his sleep, looking incredibly angelic with his dark curls and fan-shaped lashes. Rocco's expression of sheer, unconcealed wonderment filled Amber with enormous pride, but there was no denying that she was in a stupor of shock at the way matters appeared to be panning out.

Like a man in a dream, Rocco was slowly sinking down to crouch by the side of the cot so that he could get an even closer look at his sleeping son. 'The throw-back gene didn't get him,' he muttered absently.

'Sorry?'

'His hair is dark. He's not going to get the life teased out of him at school as I did,' Rocco extended with pronounced satisfaction. 'He has my nose and your mouth.'

Amber nodded in silence at news that was not news to her, but which she had not expected him to pick up on quite so quickly.

'Also my brows—'

'He got your eyes too.' Amber was in a total daze. Where were the doors slamming in her face, the denials of paternity, the demands for birth certificates, DNA testing and all the other supporting evidence she had somehow expected? Well, maybe not all of that, but at least one or two elements, she conceded dizzily.

'Where was Freddy when I was stalking you in the woods?' Rocco murmured.

She explained about her sister's nanny.

'Freddy is *really* something else,' Rocco declared of his son.

'He won the beautiful baby competition at the village fête last summer,' Amber heard herself saying with pride. 'Opal was furious and couldn't hide it. She was expecting her daughter…my niece, Chloe, to win.'

Rocco sprang fluidly upright again and cast her a veiled appraisal. 'We need to talk.'

CHAPTER NINE

ROCCO only walked to the big landing above the stairs and cast open a door there.

'You've accepted Freddy's yours, haven't you?' Amber enquired nervously. 'He's a year old next week but he was born prematurely... I had an awful pregnancy.'

'How awful?'

Scanning the spacious bedroom as he switched on the lights, Amber wondered why they weren't going downstairs again and asked.

'I want to hear Freddy if he wakes up.' Rocco studied her with stunning dark golden eyes. 'Awful... you were saying?'

'Well, I wasn't exactly fighting fit to begin with,' she pointed out, edgily pacing away from him. 'I was sick morning, noon and night as well, so I lost more weight. I couldn't find another job and I couldn't afford the rent on my flat either, so I had to move into a bedsit. I didn't have blood running in my veins by that stage, I only had stress.'

She spun back. Rocco was really pale, his bone-structure rigid.

'Had enough yet?' Amber prompted.

'No...' he framed doggedly.

'Well, my blood pressure was too high and I ended

up in hospital because I was threatening to miscarry. So there I was flat on my back and not allowed to do anything for weeks on end. It was like a living nightmare. No privacy, no visitors, no nothing, just me and my thoughts—'

'What about your sister?'

'If you knew Opal like I know Opal, you wouldn't have been in any desperate hurry to contact her and confront her with your messy mistakes either.' Amber sighed. 'But I finally had to call her because I needed my bedsit cleared out and she was really wonderful.'

'And I was nowhere—'

'I started hating you in that hospital bed,' Amber admitted.

'Am I allowed to ask why you didn't contact me?'

Amber surveyed him in outrage. 'After you accused me of stalking you?'

'Did you know you were pregnant at that stage?'

'No.'

Rocco just closed his eyes and swung away. 'I was a bastard. On Saturday, you said I wouldn't discuss that newspaper story and that that wasn't fair. You were right, so let's get it out of the way now and then never talk about it again.'

Unprepared for that subject to be raised, Amber groaned. 'I went to school with the journalist who wrote that story.'

In astonishment, Rocco froze. 'You went to *school*—'

'With Dinah Fletcher, yes.' Amber explained how the other woman had contacted her. 'She said she had only recently moved to London to start a PR job—'

'A *PR* job—?'

Amber kept on talking. 'She was always great fun at school and I was delighted to hear from her. She came over with a bottle of wine. I told her about you but I never gave her a single intimate detail. It was girly gossip, nothing more—'

Rocco sank down heavily on the foot of the bed. 'She got in touch with you because she already knew that I was seeing you. She set you up,' he breathed in a raw undertone.

'Yeah and I fell for it.' Amber could feel the tears threatening because she still felt sick at the awareness that she had actually enjoyed that evening. She had had no suspicion that Dinah was a junior reporter, ambitious to make her mark, regardless of who got hurt in the process. 'A couple of days after the story appeared, she phoned and said she hoped that there were no hard feelings and that she was only doing her job. I asked her if it was also her job to tell lies about what I'd said but she just put the phone down on me.'

Rocco viewed her with haunted dark eyes and vented a distinctly hollow laugh. 'I was planning to tell you tonight that I was now big enough to take a joke—and that at least you hadn't informed the world that I was lousy in bed and you had to fake it all the time…' His deep, dark drawl faltered. 'Now I don't know what I can say.'

'Not a lot in your own defence,' Amber agreed in a flat little tone, but the most appalling desire to surge across the room and put her arms round him was tugging at her. He was badly shaken and suddenly she was no longer feeling vengeful satisfaction. Only as she saw that within herself did she appreciate that she had so badly wanted revenge. The nasty part of her had enjoyed hammering him with all the bad news.

'I was naive…I was indiscreet and probably I deserved to get dumped because I caused you so much embarrassment,' Amber conceded in a sudden rush. 'But it was the way you *did* it—'

Brilliant dark eyes shimmering, Rocco sprang upright again. 'I was on the brink of asking you to marry me. Then that sleazy article hit me in the face and I really thought you'd been taking me for a ride!'

Amber's feet had frozen to the carpet. It was her turn to go into shock.

'Nothing had ever hurt me so much and I couldn't face seeing you again. I saw no point,' Rocco admitted heavily. 'I could see no circumstances in which that story could've been conceived without your willing agreement and participation.'

Amber stared at him with shaken eyes. 'You were going to ask me to marry you?'

Rocco pushed a not quite steady hand through his bright silvery fair hair and shrugged, but it was a jerky movement that lacked his usual grace. 'I felt you'd made such a fool of me. There I was ready to ask you to be my wife... I was in the process of buying a house, I even had the engagement ring...and then *bang*! It all fell apart in my hands.'

'But couldn't you have once stopped and thought that I wouldn't have done such a thing to you?' Amber pressed helplessly, if anything even more aghast at the discovery that she had lost so much more than she had ever dreamt. Rocco had loved her, planned to marry her. Rocco would have been pleased about Freddy. Rocco would have been there for her every wretched step of the way had not that newspaper story destroyed his faith in her.

'When I'm hurt I lash out and nothing I can do or say can alter the past. You will say I didn't love you enough...I would say I loved you *so* much, I was afraid of being weak and ending up back with you again,' Rocco bit out in a roughened undertone.

'Would you?' A glimmer of silver lining appeared in

the grey clouds that had been encircling Amber until he spoke those final words. 'And all those other women?' she asked on the strike-while-the-iron's-hot principle.

'Anything to take my mind off you and it didn't work. I didn't sleep with anyone else for a very long time... and that was lousy too. In fact...' Rocco hesitated and then forced himself on, dark blood rising to accentuate his carved cheekbones. 'Everything was lousy until I looked out Harris Winton's front window and saw you and felt alive again for the first time since I dumped you.'

'I just love you saying that when you couldn't *wait* to phone the man and talk me out of my job!' Amber exclaimed, and then her shoulders slumped, the stress and strain of it all suddenly closing in on her, making her realise all at once how absolutely exhausted she was. 'I'm almost asleep standing up.'

'You should be in bed.' Never in her life had she seen a guy leap so fast for an escape route, or at least she thought that until Rocco lifted her up into his arms and carted her over to the divan and settled her down on it with pronounced care and absolutely none of his usual familiarities.

'Are you staying?' she asked in a small tense voice.

'Not if you don't want me.'

Her teeth gritted. 'Is this your bed?'

Rocco nodded slowly.

'OK...you can stay so I can nag at you until I fall asleep,' she muttered.

'I can live with that.'

Filching a rarely worn nightdress from her case, she headed into the bathroom. Her head felt as if it were spinning with the number of conflicting thoughts assailing her, but one emotion dominated. She loved him. It didn't stop her wanting to kick him but she couldn't bear to leave him alone with his guilty conscience. Regret was just eating him alive and furthermore, on a purely practical side, Rocco was telling her things that torture wouldn't have extracted from him eighteen months ago. If he wanted to talk more, she didn't want to miss out on a single syllable. So he had planned to surprise her with a house and an engagement ring? Rocco and his blasted surprises! If only she had known, she would've crashed into his office in a tank and pinned him down to make him listen to her eighteen months ago.

She crept into bed, wondering if the nightie was overkill, but she knew that taking it off would be noticed. She listened to him undress.

'How do you feel about getting married on Christmas Eve?'

Amber blinked and then came up over the edge of the duvet to stare at the male ostensibly entranced in the shape of his own shirt buttons, but so tense she was anything but fooled. Her heart hit the Big Dipper and kept on hurtling higher. Well, he had his flaws *but*…

'Christmas Eve?' Amber echoed rather croakily. 'Well, I'm not doing anything else…'

'Like I said to you before, you won't regret it.'

It sounded like a blood oath. 'What about you?'

'I get you as my wife,' Rocco murmured, smooth as silk. 'I also get part-ownership on Freddy. Those facts will then become the only things in my life I don't have to feel bad about.'

'You're just killing me with your enthusiasm.'

'How much enthusiasm am I allowed to show?'

'Major moving on to maximum,' Amber muttered, leaning heavily on the encouragement angle. 'Fireworks, Fourth of July, whatever feels right.'

'Would you have married me eighteen months ago?'

She would have left a smoke trail in her haste to get to the church. 'Possibly…'

Rocco slid into bed. She was waiting on him mentioning love; she was praying on him mentioning love.

'You were such a workaholic then that we hardly saw each other,' Rocco remarked tautly, dimming the lights but not putting them out.

'It was such a boring job too—'

Rocco took her aback by hauling her across the bed into his arms and studying her with scorching dark golden eyes of disbelief. 'You put that *boring* job ahead of me every time!'

Amber winced, shimmied confidingly into the hard heat and muscularity of his big, powerful body and whispered softly, 'But I surrendered my wheelbarrow for you, didn't I?'

He captured her animated face between long brown fingers, gazing down into dancing green eyes that had miraculously lost the dulled look of exhaustion. 'Not without argument, *cara*.'

'I had Freddy's security to consider.' She shivered against him, drowning in the sexy depths of his stunning eyes.

'Of course…' Something cool in Rocco's agreement, a dry note, tugged anxious strings deep down in her mind, but then Rocco possessed her mouth with a raw and hungry sensual force that electrified her. He took precisely ten ruthless seconds to remove the nightdress.

'Are you angry with me?' Amber whispered, sensing a tension in him that troubled her and easing back with a furrowed brow.

'With myself…*only* with myself,' Rocco swore with roughened fervour, his spectacular gaze resting with an intensity she could feel but no longer read on her anxious face.

She edged back to him, weak not only with hunger but also with a desperate need for reassurance that everything was all right. It felt so much *more* than all right to her. She was so happy she could have cried. She didn't want him to be angry with himself. But he curved an exploring hand over the straining rosy bud crowning one pouting breast and, that fast, she was sucked down into a place where thinking was more than she could manage.

It was as though the stressful day had built up an incredibly urgent need in both of them. There was a wildness in Rocco, a wildness that was gloriously thrilling and fired her every response to fresh heights. He slid down over her quivering length, pausing to make passionate love to every promising curve and hollow he encountered in his path. Before very long, all she was remotely aware of was the thunderous crash of her own heartbeat, her breath sobbing in her throat and a level of sensation which seemed to transcend earthly existence.

'I want this to be amazing…' Rocco rasped.

She was half out of her mind with an intensity of pleasure at that point, which made it impossible to tell him that amazing did not *begin* to cover the excitement of what he was making her feel. Writhing with utterly mindless and tormented delight, she moaned his name like a mantra, clutched at his hair, grabbed his shoulders and surrendered to her own abandonment while being pleasured within an inch of her life.

'Amazing…' she managed when she could speak again but only just.

'It's not over yet,' Rocco husked in a tone of promise.

And if the beginning and the middle had been totally enthralling for her, the conclusion was an even more ecstatic and long-drawn-out affair. In the aftermath she was too weak to do anything but lie in his arms. She had a dazed sense of having seen, experienced and revisited paradise more than once and she was awash with tender love and wonderment that he was finally, actually and for ever hers.

That was the inopportune moment when Rocco shifted away from her and breathed flatly like a male to whom paradise was an utterly unknown place, 'At least I know you're not faking it now…'

I'm not going to say anything, screeched the alarm-bell voice inside her shaken head. She hadn't got the energy for a row, she told herself weakly, and she curved into a comfy pillow like a hampster burrowing into a hiding place. They could row *after* they got married.

CHAPTER TEN

AMBER focused on her own reflection in the cheval dressing mirror.

It was Christmas Eve and it was her wedding day and she was wearing the most divine dress she had ever seen or ever worn. The delicate gold-and-silver-embroidered boned bodice hugged her to the waist, where the full ivory rustling skirt flared out, overlaid at the back by an elaborate train with matching embroidery. She pointed her toes to see her satin shoes adorned with tulle roses, tipped up her chin the better to allow the light catch the superb contemporary gold and diamond tiara and the elegant short veil that hung in a flirty froth from the back of her head.

But it was no use! No matter how hard Amber tried to lose herself in bridal fervour, she had to emerge again to be confronted by an awful truth: Rocco *wasn't* happy! She was wilfully marrying a man who didn't love her, but who very much wanted to be a father to their son. Her nose tickled as she fought to hold back welling tears. It had honestly not occurred to her until after she had said yes to his marriage proposal that his most likely motivation had been sheer guilt and Freddy.

It had been days since Rocco had even kissed her—not since that very first night. The next day, she had returned from her shopping trip for her wedding outfit and a slight difference of opinion had resulted in her hot-headedly transferring her possessions into the guest room next to Freddy's. She had kind of shot herself in the foot with that relocation: Rocco had neither come in search of her nor betrayed the slightest awareness of the reality that she had gone missing from his bed. Separate bedrooms and they weren't even married yet, she thought wretchedly. Just when she had believed that every cloud on her horizon had vanished, a brick-wall barrier had come up out of nowhere and divided them. Since then Rocco could not have made it clearer that Freddy was his biggest source of interest.

He had spent that whole day with Freddy while she'd been shopping. When she'd got back, Freddy had been in his bath. Rocco had been dive-bombing Freddy's toy boats with pretty much the same enjoyment that Freddy got from loads of noisy splashes and sound effects, but her entrance to the fun and frolics had cast a distinct dampener on the proceedings.

'Did you find a dress?' he asked with scrupulous politeness.

'Yes…it cost a fortune. Thanks,' she said with the semi-guilty, semi-euphoric response of a woman who had managed to locate her dream wedding gown, her dream veil and her dream shoes, not to mention a set of lingerie that had quite taken her breath away.

'Odd how being a kept woman within marriage doesn't seem to bother you quite the way it bothered you *before* I mentioned the wedding ring,' Rocco drawled in a black-velvet purr.

Screening her shaken and hurt eyes at that cutting comment, which she was absolutely defenceless against, Amber murmured, 'Would you like me to go and mow the lawn to justify my existence?'

'You picked me up wrong, *cara…*'

Like heck, she had misunderstood! So that was why she had shifted into a guest room but doing that had made it even easier for Rocco to distance himself from her. There he was surging home every evening to spend time with Freddy, perfectly charming and polite with her, but the instant Freddy had fallen asleep, Rocco had excused himself to work. It was as if they had already been married ninety years and he had nothing left to say to her!

Amber straightened her bowed shoulders, took a last longing, lingering look at her reflection in her dream wedding gown and faced facts. Nearly all week, she had refused to let go of her fantasy of becoming Rocco's wife. Hiding her head in the sand, she had shrunk from acknowledging that Rocco was showing as much enthusiasm for matrimony as the proverbial condemned man.

She could ring him on his mobile before he arrived at the church. Better a misfired wedding than the misery of a marriage that was a mistake, she told herself. Blinking back tears, Amber stabbed out his number and waited for Rocco to answer.

'Rocco? Where are you?'

'*En route* to the church. What's wrong?'

'I want to call it off,' Amber whispered.

'Call…what off?' Rocco breathed jerkily.

Amber gulped. 'I don't think we should go through with the wedding. You've been so unhappy for days—'

'And *this* is the magic cure? I'm a bloody sight *more* unhappy now!' Rocco launched down the line at her with incredulous force. 'You've got cold feet, that's all. Now pull yourself together. We're getting married today!'

'But you don't really want to marry me—'

'Where did you get that idea? I really, really, *really* want to marry you,' Rocco murmured intensely, changing both tack and volume. 'I want to be stalked by you every day for the rest of my life—'

'But you couldn't even stalk *me* as far as one of your own guest rooms!' A sob caught at Amber's voice.

'Cards on the table time,' Rocco muttered with fierce urgency. 'I somehow got the impression that you were only marrying me for Freddy's benefit—'

'Don't be stupid…' Amber winced and then confided in a small voice, 'Actually I was thinking the same thing about you.'

'Freddy's wonderful, but he's not so wonderful that I'd sentence myself to a lifetime with a woman I didn't want,' Rocco swore impressively.

'I also thought that maybe you were just marrying me because you felt guilty—'

'No, I think most guys run the other way if they feel *that* guilty. I can handle guilt, but I'm not at all sure I can handle not having you…'

Amber blossomed from a nervous wreck into a happy bride-to-be again. 'See you at the church—'

'You've made me really nervous now—'

'Well, you shouldn't have ignored me for so long in favour of Freddy,' Amber told him dulcetly.

Neville was waiting downstairs to accompany her. Opal had arrived with her husband early that morning to help Amber into her bridal regalia and had then gone on to the church in company with Freddy and Freddy's new nanny, a lovely friendly girl, whom Rocco had insisted on hiring to help Amber.

Amber negotiated the stairs with the housekeeper holding up her train. Her brother-in-law gave her a smiling appraisal. 'You look incredible, Amber. Rocco won't know what's hit him.'

Amber rather thought Rocco *would* know what had hit him after that emotional phone call they had shared.

They were each as bad as the other, she reflected ruefully. Neither of them had shared their deepest fears over the past few days. She had been pretty tough on Rocco that first night in London. But she was really surprised that a male as confident as he was had entertained the lowering suspicion that she might only be marrying him for Freddy's benefit and for security. Somehow, she recognised, she had subconsciously assumed that Rocco *knew* she was still madly in love with him. Now she knew he *didn't* know and was amazingly subject to the same insecurities as she was. A sunny smile spread over her face at that acknowledgement.

The church was absolutely miles away, right outside London. Amber thought Rocco had picked a very inconvenient location but then she had had nothing to do with *any* of the arrangements: Rocco had assured her that he had everything organised. Feeling that he could at least have consulted her about her own wedding day, she had rigorously refused to ask questions.

The Rolls finally drew up outside a charming rural church surrounded by cars. As Amber got out her emergence and her progress into the church were minutely recorded by a busy bunch of men wielding all sorts of cameras. The press? she wondered in surprise. Then she looked down the aisle and saw Rocco waiting for her at the altar and all such minor musings evaporated. There he was, six feet four inches of devastatingly handsome masculinity, and her heart started racing. She might have generously offered him his freedom back, but she had never been so grateful to have an offer refused.

Stunning dark golden eyes scanned her, stilled and just stayed locked to her all the way down the aisle. It wasn't at all cool bridegroom behaviour, but Amber loved that poleaxed stare. He didn't have to speak: she knew he thought she looked spectacular. He reached for her hand at the altar. She was so happy that her eyes stung a little. The plain and simple words of the ceremony sounded beautiful to her. Freddy, however, let out an anguished wail at the sight of both his mother and his father disappearing out of view to sign the wedding register. Amber darted back to retrieve their anxious son from his nanny's knee and take him with them.

'You look incredibly gorgeous,' Rocco told her as he lifted Freddy from her arms to give him a consoling hug. Back where he felt he ought to be in the very centre of things, Freddy smiled.

Loads of photos were taken on the church steps and Rocco swept her off into the waiting limo as soon as he could.

Amber gave him a teasing look. 'Do you think you could tell me now where we're having our reception?'

'Wychwood House.'

A slight frown-line indented her brow. 'I've heard that name before somewhere.'

'Let me jog your memory.' A wolfish grin was now tugging at the corners of Rocco's expressive mouth. 'When we were together last year, do you remember the way you always used to devour the property sections of the Sunday newspapers?'

A slow tide of hot pink crept up over Amber's face, but she lifted her brows in apparent surprise. 'No…'

'Married an hour and already lying to me,' Rocco reproved with vibrant amusement. 'Did you think I didn't notice that while I was deep in the business news you were enjoying a covert thrill scanning the houses for sale?'

Feeling very much as though an embarrassing secret habit had been exposed, Amber bristled defensively. 'Well, just glancing through the property pages is not a crime, is it?'

'Just glancing?' Rocco flung his handsome head back and laughed out loud at that understatement. 'You were in seventh heaven rustling through those pages. So when you finally went to the lengths of removing an entire page from a newspaper, I knew it was a fair bet that you'd found your dream house.'

Just then, Amber recalled ripping out that particular page while Rocco had been in the shower. A sudden, barely considered impulse after reading an interesting article about the history of a gorgeous country house that had been about to come on to the market.

'So after doing some investigation to find out which house it was, I bought it for you.'

'Honestly?' Amber was going off into shock. 'B-but I thought it was the house in London that you bought for us last year!'

'No, that was a much more recent acquisition. I bought Wychwood for you a week before we broke up.'

'But…' Amber was just transfixed with disbelief.

'I told you that I had a country estate,' Rocco reminded her gently.

Recalling the context in which that statement had been made and taken by her as a most unfunny joke on her gardening status, Amber swallowed with difficulty. By then the Rolls was already powering up an imposing winding drive that led through a long sweep of beautiful rolling parkland adorned by mature oak trees.

'Not all my surprises go wrong, tabbycat,' Rocco commented with the kind of rich self-satisfaction that she usually set out to squash flat in him.

However, as the magnificent Palladian mansion came into view round the next bend Amber was too dumbstruck to do anything other than nod agreement in slow motion.

'Although I have to confess that this particular surprise felt like it had gone *very* wrong when I got

Wychwood without you included,' Rocco confided ruefully.

In normal mode, Amber would have told him that that was the direct result of his having dumped her and that he had deserved to have had his surprise backfire on him. But the truth was she was so thunderstruck by the sheer size of the house *and* the surprise, she was feeling generous.

Rocco lifted her out of the Rolls and up into his arms. It was just as well: she honestly didn't believe her legs would have held her up. 'Rocco…?'

She collided with dark golden eyes that filled her to overflowing with joyful tenderness and what felt fearfully like adoration, so she didn't tell him she loved him, she said instead, 'I think you're totally wonderful.'

Was it her imagination or did he look a little disappointed?

'Absolutely fantastic…the most terrific husband in the world?' she added in a rush.

Evidently she finally struck the right note of appreciation because he took her mouth with hungry, plundering intensity. As excitement charged her every skin-cell, she realised just how miserably long a few days without Rocco's passion could feel.

'Incredibly sexy too,' she mumbled, coming up for air again as he carried her over the impressive threshold of Wychwood House.

A towering Christmas tree festooned with ornaments and beautiful twinkling lights took pride of place in the wonderful reception hall where a log fire burned. 'Oh, my…' she whispered, appreciation growing by the second. 'Rocco, please, please tell me we're going to spend Christmas here.'

He smiled. 'The day after Boxing Day, we set off for warmer climes.'

All the photographers then sprang out from behind the tree to take loads more pictures of them and she tried not to let her jaw drop too obviously. 'Really conscientious, aren't they?' she whispered to Rocco when they had to stop to load more film.

'I told them I didn't want a single second of this day to go unrecorded.'

Freddy was belatedly fetched out of the Rolls where he had been abandoned because he was fast asleep. Reunited with his nanny when she arrived, he was borne upstairs to complete his nap in greater comfort and Rocco and Amber were free to greet their guests. Some of them she had met when she'd been seeing Rocco the previous year. Others were strangers. And then there were the Wintons: Harris coming as close to a grin when he wished her well as he was ever likely to come, and Kaye with her gutsy smile, not one whit perturbed by any memory of having warned Amber off Rocco only a week earlier.

Neville and Opal joined them at the top table in the elegant dining room where the caterers served a magnificent meal. Amber watched for Rocco getting that glazed look men usually got around Opal, but if he was susceptible he was very good at concealing it.

'My sister's very beautiful, isn't she?' Amber was reduced to fishing for an opinion when they were walking through to the ballroom where a band was playing.

'Do I get shot if I say no...or shot if I say yes?' Rocco teased.

Amber coloured hotly at his insight into her feelings.

Rocco curved an arm round her taut shoulders in a soothing gesture. 'She's lovely and very fond of you, but I have to confess that listening to her talk to you as if you are a very small and not very bright child is extremely irritating.'

Amber paled.

'Now what have I said? You know you rarely mention your family—'

She forced a rueful laugh. 'My parents were very clever, just like Opal—'

'Research scientists. I remember you telling me that.'

'By their standards I *wasn't* very bright. I'm average but they made me feel stupid,' Amber admitted reluctantly. 'I felt I was such a disappointment to them—'

'So that's why you always pushed yourself so hard. If your parents had seen how hard you'd worked and how much you had achieved by the time I met you, they would have been hugely impressed,' Rocco swore vehemently.

'You sound like you really mean that, *but* I remember you offering me employment and behaving as if the job I had was nothing—'

'Give me a break.' Rocco laughed softly. The protective tenderness in his gaze warmed her like summer sunlight. 'All I was thinking of was being able to see more of you and you *were* wasted in the position you were in then.'

Amber stood up on tiptoe and whispered playfully, 'Go on, tell me more, tell me how bright I am—'

Rocco caught her to him with a strong arm, making her urgently aware of him and the glinting gold of his smouldering scrutiny. 'You picked me didn't you?'

'Is that really one of the brighter moves I've made?'

Rocco looked down into her animated face and murmured with ragged fervour, 'I hope so because I love you like crazy, *bella mia*.'

Amber stilled. 'Honestly?'

'Why are you looking so shocked?'

She linked her arms round his neck and sighed helplessly. 'You let me go, Rocco...you never came after me—'

A dark rise of colour had accentuated his fabulous cheekbones. 'I *did* come after you. It took me two months to get to that point. Two months of sleepless nights and hating every other woman because she wasn't you. I told myself I just wanted to confront you...which is pretty much what I told myself when I saw you with your wheelbarrow as well—'

'You *did* come after me?' Amber gasped in delight, finally willing to believe he might still truly love her. 'So why didn't you find me?'

'You'd moved out of your flat without leaving a forwarding address and I had no relatives or anyone else to contact,' Rocco ground out in frustration. 'I even got a friend to run your Social Security number through a computer search system...that's illegal, but it didn't turn up anything helpful.'

'I forgive you for everything...I love you, I love you, I love you!' Amber told him, bouncing up and down on the spot, so intense was her happiness and excitement.

'For goodness' sake, Amber...remember where you are,' Opal's voice interposed in pained and mortified reproof.

'She's in her own home and I'm enjoying this tremendously, Opal. If you'll excuse us,' Rocco murmured with a brilliant smile as he whirled his ebullient bride onto the floor to open the dancing.

At three in the morning, Amber and Rocco came downstairs with Freddy to open some Christmas presents.

Freddy was in the best of good humour. It was Christmas Day and it was also his first birthday. He was truly aware of neither occasion but was enthralled by

the big tree and all the twinkly lights and the shiny ornaments. He played with the card he was given and he
played with the wrapping paper, watching while his
parents struggled to get the elephant rocker out of its
box, and then struggled even more on the discovery
that it was only part-assembled. He sat in the rocker for
about one minute before crawling off it again to head
for the much more exciting box he wanted to explore.

'I think the rocker just bombed,' Rocco groaned.
'He's happier with the paper and the packaging.'

'As long as he's happy, who cares?' Amber said
sunnily, entranced in watching the lights send fire glittering from the superb diamond engagement ring Rocco
had slid onto her finger. 'I bet I'm the only bride for
miles around who got an engagement ring *after* the
wedding and it's really gorgeous!'

'Just arriving eighteen months late, tabbycat.' Rocco
surveyed her with loving but amused eyes as she
whooped over the matching eternity ring she had just
unwrapped. 'That's for suffering all those weeks in
hospital to have Freddy.'

'Well, perhaps it wasn't as bad as I made out…if I'd
had you visiting, I'm sure I wouldn't have been feeling
sorry for myself. Next time—'

'*Next* time? Are you kidding?' Rocco exclaimed in
horror. 'Freddy's going to be an only child!'

As Freddy had crawled into the box and now
couldn't get out of the box and was behaving very much
as if the box were attacking him, Amber rescued him
and put him back on the rocker. After that disturbing experience, the elephant's quieter charms were more appreciated.

'I'll be fine the next time,' Amber told him sooth-
ingly.

'I love Freddy, but I value your health more, *bella mia*.'

'Yes…you worship the ground I walk on,' Amber reminded him chattily as she measured the huge pile of presents still awaiting her and looked at Freddy and Rocco, especially Rocco. Rocco who was so incredibly romantic and passionate and hers now. Rocco winced. 'Did I say that?'

'And lots of other things too…you got quite carried away around midnight.' Confident as only a woman who knew she was loved could be, Amber gave him a glorious, wicked smile.

Rocco entwined his fingers round hers and hauled her back to him with possessive hands. 'You're a witch and I adore you—'

'I adore you too…so I didn't buy you the book on how to pleasure a woman in two hundred ways in case you thought I was dropping hints,' she said teasingly. 'I mean, I might die of exhaustion if I got any more pleasure. So I got you this instead. Merry Christmas, Rocco.'

Rocco unwrapped his miniature gold wheelbarrow and dealt her a vibrant grin of appreciation, which just turned her heart over. 'I'll keep it on my desk, *cara*.'

Freddy was slumped asleep over the elephant's head.

'You and Freddy are the best Christmas presents I have ever had,' Rocco confided with touching sincerity as he cradled his gently snoring son.

'Well, I did even better,' Amber pointed out, resting back beneath his other arm, blissfully content as she stared into the glowing embers of the fire. 'I got you, a fantastic wedding and this is going to be the most wonderful Christmas because it's our first together—'

Rocco urged her round to him and claimed her mouth in a sweet, delicious kiss that left her melting into his hard, muscular frame. 'Magical,' he groaned hungrily, and only Freddy's snuffly little complaint about being squashed got them back upstairs again.